SUNNY DAYS FOR SAM

Other Books by Jennifer Shirk

Georgie on His Mind

SUNNY DAYS FOR SAM

•

Jennifer Shirk

AVALON BOOKS
NEW YORK

Published by Avalon Books,
an imprint of Thomas Bouregy & Co., Inc.
New York, NY

Library of Congress Cataloging-in-Publication Data

Shirk, Jennifer.
  Sunny days for Sam / Jennifer Shirk.
  p. cm.
  ISBN 978-0-8034-7468-0 (hardcover : acid-free paper)
1. Young women—Fiction.   I. Title.
  PS3619.H593S86 2012
  813'.6—dc23

                                            2011040000

PRINTED IN THE UNITED STATES OF AMERICA
ON ACID-FREE PAPER
BY RR DONNELLEY, HARRISONBURG, VIRGINIA

F

For all the wonderful and supportive women at The Passionate Critters Critique group. I wouldn't have this book (or my sanity) if it wasn't for you all. Thanks for your friendship as well as your critiques. You ladies rock!

Chapter One

Lifting the hem of her heavily laced gown, Sunny Fletcher looked down at her swollen feet and thought, *If I were Cinderella, I would've smacked that Fairy Godmother upside the head.* The extravagant princess ensemble Sunny had on didn't include glass slippers, but that didn't mean she couldn't sympathize with Cinderella's foot-aching plight any less. Sunny's slippers were made of rock-hard plastic, and the teeny-tiny straps cut into her ankles every time she shifted her footing. Unfortunately, she had to squelch any godmother-thrashing desire she might have had at the moment. She had a job to do. She needed to remember that, and she rallied an enthusiastic smile for the camera.

Cinderella would have been proud.

Sunny kept the smile pasted on her face even after Bud, the photographer, snapped the picture, then double-checked the outcome. When he appeared satisfied enough with the result, he clasped his hands together and smiled pleasantly to the long line of children waiting for their pictures to be taken.

"Okay, kids, Princess Miranda is going to take a short

break and head off to . . . uh, her castle," Bud announced. "Don't worry, the royal cat, Chow Chow, will be available until she gets back."

A loud groan emanated from the crowd—more from the parents who had waited in the humid heat than from the children. Sunny bit her lip and thought of foregoing her break for them, but the snow-cone girl had cinched her dress too tightly, and she needed to have it fixed before she passed out. She tried not to hobble as she moved away from the children. These shoes were going to be the demise of her, for sure. But what could she really expect? A pair of Naturalizer pumps? If Cinderella's godmother couldn't be thoughtful enough to provide a comfortable pair of heels for a princess dancing all night, then Sunny had no right to think the owners of Fairytale Land Amusement Park would give them to a princess standing on her feet for eight hours.

But she wouldn't complain. *Couldn't* complain. Jobs in town were scarce now, and since her grandmother had passed away, she needed the money more than ever.

Sunny shot Bud a grateful smile. Thank goodness *somebody* in this amusement park was on her swollen-feet side. As she stepped behind the photo curtain, she took off one of her long satin gloves and dabbed her cheeks and forehead with it, careful not to smudge her makeup. It was hotter than Hades at the Jersey shore today, unusually so this early in the summer season.

"Oh, Princess Miranda!" she heard someone call.

Sunny peered over her shoulder and saw her boss, Mr. Twardski, weaving through the crowd. When he finally reached her—doing some heavy panting and sweating of his own—he pulled out a handkerchief from his back pocket and mopped his bald head as he caught his breath.

Still playing the part of princess in front of any passerby customers, Sunny genuflected in greeting. But her crown inadvertently slipped and hung on her left ear, ruining her attempt at gracefulness. She reached up and tried to straighten her crown. She wished she had remembered to secure it with bobby pins. Hairspray was something she didn't own either, and now she was paying for it. In this humid summer weather, her straight blond hair was probably going to get flatter and straighter by the hour.

"What is it, Mr. Twardski?" She blew her damp bangs out of her eyes. "I was just about to take my break."

"Yeah, I know," he said, his eyes taking on a familiar gleam that put her on high alert. "Sure is hot today, isn't it?"

Sunny just stared at him. Was he joking? Of course it was hot! She looked like she'd just taken a leisurely stroll through a car wash. Twice.

Her boss nodded at her silence. "Well, I wanted to tell ya that Kenny's got a nice big pitcher of lemonade waiting in the office. Made it himself. Personally."

Ugh. She tried not to make a face, but she'd rather die of thirst.

Kenny was Mr. Twardski's son. She'd known him since high school. Unfortunately, not much about the arrogant weasel had changed in five years. Kenny was always staring at her for too long or standing way too close. She also didn't appreciate how he'd go out of his way to remind her that he was her boss' son and that she should treat him with extra respect.

She didn't want to hedge a guess as to what the lecher's definition of *extra respect* was. "Kenny is . . ." She cleared her throat and avoided eye contact, hoping her tone would sound polite and not snippy. "Wow, that's so thoughtful."

Mr. Twardski took her elbow and gently started leading her toward the managerial office. "He's waiting in there for ya," he said with a wink, then tipped his chin toward the door.

I bet. Her shoulders wilted, and she felt her crown slip to her ear again. *Wonderful.* The last thing she wanted to do was spend her break fighting off Kenny Twardski. Her feet hurt enough. She didn't need to go and add a headache to her ailments.

"Um, you know what?" she said, removing her boss' hand from her arm. "I have to use the restroom. Oh, and I should see what I can do with this hair of mine too. I'm not really thirsty anyway." As soon as the words left her mouth, she winced.

Uh-oh. She'd been home free and clear until she'd said that last part about not being thirsty. Of course she was thirsty! What person standing out in this heat for more than thirty seconds *wouldn't* be thirsty? Only an idiot would say something like that. Or a liar. And based on the narrow-eyed expression of her boss, it looked as if he'd just figured out how big of an idiot-liar she was.

"Miss Sunny, I'm beginning to think you're trying to avoid my Kenny. He's got a nice drink in there for ya, and suddenly you're not thirsty? Just last week he had a dinner waitin', and you said you weren't hungry."

Ooops. Busted. "Oh, uh, well, it's not that—"

"Shame on you. After all I did for you, you gotta go and treat my son like some ditch-digger with leprosy."

She blinked. Well, she wouldn't go *that* far. Guilt suddenly spread over her, hot and thick—much like today's weather. She supposed it wouldn't have killed her to have one sip of his son's dumb lemonade. Mom-mom would have been disappointed in her manners. Mr. Twardski was good to her for giving her work when he could have hired a younger girl for cheaper pay. She didn't want to hurt Mr. Twardski's feelings either. After all, he didn't know what a jerk his son was.

"Kenny's a good man," her boss went on. "He's got a good job too. Your grandmother would have been tickled pink to know you and my son had somehow gotten together. If you'd give him a chance, you could even be married."

Her head jerked back so hard, her crown flew off. "*Married?*"

Mr. Twardski's crinkled features remained calm at her outburst as he took his pipe out of his shirt pocket and waved it under his nose. "That's right. And I'll be honest, my Kenny has been sweet on you for years. He'd be good to you too. Help you."

She placed a hand over her stomach. Puking didn't seem that far off at the thought of becoming *Mrs.* Kenny Twardski.

"*Help* me?" she squeaked.

Her boss leaned in, and she was hit hard with the smell of tobacco and coffee. The odor compounded the queasiness already swirling in her stomach. "Yeah. My Kenny could help you with . . . your debt," he whispered.

Her shoulders tensed. The truth in his words stung her pride, but she was struck harder by surprise. She wasn't aware that anyone in town knew of the debt she had because of Mom-mom's medical bills. Bad news apparently traveled fast.

She had always called her grandmother Mom-mom, since she was the closest thing to a mother she'd had. Sunny's real mom had died giving birth to her. Sunny's dad had been unable to care for her and had eventually signed over custody to her grandmother when Sunny was six months old. They'd had a wonderful life together until cancer took Mom-mom only a short year ago.

Sunny had dropped out of college to care for her, and since they didn't have medical insurance, she had made it a point to work any job she could get—including becoming Princess Miranda at Fairytale Land Amusement Park—to pay off the toppling mound of doctor bills.

Sunny figured she'd survived this long on her own. And despite what Mr. Twardski had just said and the bleakness of her current financial situation, her grandmother certainly wouldn't have expected her to marry a man she didn't *like,* let alone love.

Squaring her shoulders, she lifted her chin. "I'm fine, Mr. Twardski. I don't need Kenny's money. For your information, we live in the twenty-first century now. Just because I'm a woman doesn't mean I can't support myself."

Her boss' face flushed scarlet. "You watch yourself, young lady. No need to get smart. I won't tolerate it in any of my employees. Don't think I'm above getting another princess around here on short notice. You're skating on thin ice as it is with all those late arrivals of yours."

Her anger deflated, and she mentally reprimanded herself for allowing her temper to get the better of her. She'd been late to work a few times, but it had never been an issue with her boss before. She'd have to watch herself. This job was everything right now. Despite the harassment from Kenny and the wardrobe malfunctions, the pay was good. "I'm sorry, sir. It won't happen again."

"See that it doesn't." Her boss nodded stiffly and dismissed her by storming back toward the office building.

When Mr. Twardski was finally a safe distance away, Sunny breathed out a sigh of relief. He might be angry with her for turning down his *Fiddler on the Roof* style of marriage arrangement, but at least she still had her job.

Sunny bent down and picked up her crown off the ground. She checked her watch and almost wanted to cry. That awkward conversation had completely killed her break time. And she really was dying of thirst. Maybe she could slip out to the boardwalk and get an iced tea without her boss noticing.

"Yeah, I know now isn't a good time to take off, but I'm not exactly taking off. Think of it as setting up my office a few hours away. I'm even having a printer delivered tomorrow. Oh, calm down, Mark. It's only for the summer. What's that in measured time, a few weeks?" Sam Calloway switched his cell phone to his other ear and turned away from his children, who were staring him down.

"Look, I can't talk right now," he said, lowering his voice. "You'll see. Everything will be fine. We'll talk about this later." He clicked his phone off and, after a brief check for any new e-mails, turned his attention back to the twins.

"Daddy, you *pwomised* I could get my picture with the *pwincess*," his little girl whined. "And you said you should never make a *pwomise* you can't keep."

His son scrunched up his face as if he'd just smelled old gym socks. "Is she a real princess, Dad, or one of those fake ones like they have at Disney World?"

Sam rubbed the bridge of his nose and chuckled. It wasn't easy raising two precocious children. "Okay. First off, yes, Emma, we will get a picture with the princess, and second, I don't know if she's a real princess, Cole. Maybe you can ask for her credentials when you meet her."

The animated expressions on his children's faces told

him he had made the right decision in coming to the town of Ocean Bluff. His kids already seemed more at ease and better behaved. Their bad behavior had been mentioned to him at the end of the school year and by their last nanny. Sam had decided then and there that he needed to slow the pace for them and take them to a nice shore town for the summer, where they could go to the beach, swim, and enjoy the outdoors. Have some real fun—much more than they would have had if they'd stayed cooped up in their Manhattan condo.

Emma sandwiched his hand inside her two little ones and tugged. "Let's go now, Daddy. I really want to see the *pwincess.* I just know she'll be beautiful."

Sam smiled down into his daughter's anxious face. When she said the word *beautiful,* it came out sounding like *boo-tee-full.* Then he remembered he'd forgotten to return an important e-mail. "All right, sweetheart. We'll go in one more minute. Daddy needs to do just a little work first."

Cole groaned. "How long is a minute?"

"Yeah, how long is a minute?" Emma echoed.

Sam took out his phone again and scrolled down to his e-mail. "Sixty seconds."

"Awww, that'll take forever," Cole muttered.

"No, it won't." Sam chuckled. "Now just sit right over there on that bench, and as soon as I'm done, we'll go over and see Princess Miranda."

Sam didn't wait for an answer. He turned and replied to his e-mail. The kids were too young to understand how demanding his job was. He was still amazed at how quickly his company had taken off. It had all started with an idea in his friend's basement, and now, ten years later, they were responsible for creating Mambo.com, the best Internet search engine in the world. And the business was still growing. They hoped to add ten more languages to the site by the end of the year and a new office complex in San Francisco.

And here was Sam Calloway in this little shore town in New Jersey for the entire summer. It wasn't going to be easy being away from his company for so long, but with technology being what it was, he figured he could handle it. Whatever was best for his children. He hoped they liked it here. Too bad he couldn't find a new nanny to come down here and watch the kids while he worked. He'd have to make some inquiries around town about a nanny agency. Or better yet, see about a nice summer camp program that would allow him to have part of the day to himself to conduct business.

Their mother's passing hadn't been easy on them. Their problematic behavior attested to that. Sam was determined to make this time at the beach enjoyable for them. Even if he wasn't entirely happy, he was going to make damn sure his children were.

Sunny took a tenuous sip of her iced tea. It tasted delicious, but she wasn't sure how much liquid she could fit in her stomach and still be able to breathe in this princess costume. She was going to have to find someone fast to loosen it for her before the next photo session began.

She was going to be late now too. The crowd—and her boss—were going to have a fit if she didn't get back to her post. If only her feet weren't ready to snap off from these plastic slippers, she could limp over there a little faster.

She looked over at her crowded post. Bud made a face and motioned for her to move quicker. *Yeah.* Like that was going to happen. She was already walking as fast as her dress and shoes would humanly allow. Then all of a sudden she heard something through the chatter and laughter of the crowd. It sounded like crying.

A child crying.

She froze. Bud frowned at her, but the wailing nearly broke her heart. She had to try to help. She raised her index finger to signal that she'd be there in a minute and turned toward the crying.

Two children stood alone by the cotton candy stand. They looked about five—maybe six—years old. Probably brother and sister, judging by their identical red hair. The boy had his arm halfway around the crying girl and was patting her back. Sunny looked around and immediately wondered where their parents were.

"Hi there," she said to them, trying to bend down to their level. The dress wouldn't give an inch. *Who created this dress anyway?* She tried again, this time keeping her back straight and bending only at the knees so she could look them in the eyes.

The little girl stopped crying and blinked up. "*Pwincess* Miranda," she whispered in awe.

"Holy smokes!" the boy cried. "You're way prettier than Cinderella or Snow White and *almost* as pretty as Ariel."

Sunny smiled wryly. "Uh, thanks. I think." She pulled off one of her gloves and began using it as a tissue, wiping the little girl's nose and cheeks. "What's wrong, honey? Why are you crying?"

The girl blew her nose in the glove, then sniffled. "I wanted to see them make the cotton candy. But now I don't know where my daddy is." The girl's crystal blue eyes began to well up with water again.

Sunny held up her hands as if that was enough to ward

off the influx of tears. "Okay, okay. We'll find your daddy, sweetie. Don't worry."

Sunny gazed up and began searching the multitude of people, hoping to find a frantic-looking man coming their way at any second. No such luck.

"What does your daddy look like?" she asked.

The little boy swiped his nose on his sleeve and puffed out his chest. "He's really strong. He can lift me and my sister right over his head."

Well, that narrows it down. Sunny chuckled at the boy's obvious admiration for his father. "Uh, okay. But what about what he was wearing? Do you remember what color shirt he had on?"

The little girl sniffed again and nodded. "Wed."

"*Wed?*"

"She means red," the boy explained. "We're both five, but I talk gooder."

His sister punched his arm. "Do not."

He shoved her back. "Do too."

"Okay, okay. Enough, you two," Sunny said, trying to block their flailing arms. Her crown slipped off again, and she almost laughed out loud at the absurdity of the situation. "Let's just look for a man wearing wed—er, I mean *red*." *And maybe look for a police officer too.*

"Emma! Cole! Oh, thank God!" a male voice shouted.

"Daddy!" they squealed as they ran over to him.

Sunny looked up at the sky, relief running through every vein in her body. Nothing was scarier to a child than getting lost. Sunny felt her eyes well up, but she blinked back the tears before they could fall. She was struck with a hollow feeling of grief at the sudden thought of her grandmother's passing.

She missed her so much. Losing someone you love hurt at any age.

Sunny cleared her thoughts and whirled around in the family's direction, a little surprised at what she found. Unlike his children, the father had wavy dark brown hair. The man was handsome too—with a long, well-shaped nose, strong, pointed chin, and clean-shaven skin. He wore a deep red polo shirt with khaki shorts, and his nice-sized biceps showed he was in good shape without being overly muscular. A man who obviously went to the gym but not on a regular basis, she judged. Probably a busy dad.

He gave each child a big hug and kiss, but he still looked pale and shaky. "I told you to sit on the bench while I did a little work. Why did you disobey me? I thought—I was afraid something terrible had happened to you."

Sunny took that as her cue to explain. She cleared her throat and took a step closer. "Um, I believe your little girl wanted to see how they made cotton candy. At least that's the story she gave me," she said with a wink, smiling at how tightly the little girl had her arms wrapped around her father's neck.

The man's expression changed before she could blink. He looked up at her then with intense gray blue eyes, almost the color of storm clouds, and Sunny's heart clenched. What kind of storm could possibly be brewing inside such a handsome man?

"I'm sorry," he said with a polite, thin smile, "but who are you?"

"Daddy, that's *Pwincess* Miranda," his daughter explained.

"Yeah, she gave her glove to Emma, and Emma used it as a tissue. It was so gross," the boy said with a wide grin.

The father's dark eyebrows slanted into a frown. Sunny

tucked the *gross* glove behind her back and took a step away. The father's distrusting look concerned her. Suddenly she felt as if she had made a huge mistake trying to help out these two little kids.

Sunny hesitated, trying to come up with something that would appease him. She didn't know why, but she had a sneaky feeling this man wouldn't be happy with *any* answer she gave. "Um, well . . . I tried to help. All I really ended up doing was keeping them company until you found them. It wasn't a big deal. It's what any park employee would do. . . ."

He stared at her as if he was trying to come up with some psychological analysis of her statements. She fidgeted under his scrutiny and tried to straighten her crown again.

"Thank you," he said after a long moment.

Sunny gave in to a smile. She had a feeling this guy wasn't big on dishing out the compliments—especially the thank-yous. She waved his appreciation away with her snotty glove. "Oh, sure. Anytime."

Anytime?

Sure, feel free to lose your kids anytime. Sheesh! Could she sound any more dimwitted?

"I mean, I'm not implying that your kids would get lost again so soon. Or that you're not a responsible father. I'm just . . . um, you're welcome."

His expression didn't change, but she was almost sure his lips had twitched. And if she'd blinked at that precise moment, she would have missed it.

He stood up from his crouched position, his daughter still holding on to his neck with her feet dangling in the air, and held out his hand. "Nice meeting you, Princess Miranda."

She extended her arm, and his large hand automatically wrapped around hers. She found it interesting that despite the man's cold attitude, his touch was warm and welcoming. Her gaze met his then, and . . . Something sizzled inside of her, and her breath caught. She quickly pulled back her hand, alarmed at this odd sense of awareness she obviously had for this brooding father. A brooding father who wore no wedding ring. *Interesting.*

His daughter let go of his neck and dropped to her feet. "I want a hug, please," Emma said, reaching out her little arms to Sunny.

Sunny gave the man a sheepish grin and hugged his daughter. The strap of her shoes cut into her ankle again. She pulled away and lifted up her skirt, holding out her ankle to check for damage to her skin.

"Your shoes are so *pwetty*," the little girl said dreamily.

Pretty? Sunny was about to make a face, then got an idea—one that would benefit them both. "Hey, would you like a souvenir of our meeting? You can have my pretty slippers, if you'd like." At least these shoes had the potential to make *somebody* happy.

The little girl squealed with delight. "Oooh! Can I, Daddy? Can I have them?"

"*May* I have them. And I guess so," the man said, checking his watch.

Sunny tried to bend down to undo the strap of her shoe, but she heard her gown begin to tear. She stopped and looked beseechingly at him. "Uh, could you, uh, take them off for me?" She pointed to her waist. "I'm sort of constrained in here."

The man nodded and bent to her feet, but not before she saw him grin—a full-fledged, all-out grin. Aha! So the Tin Man *did* have a heart. She had begun to have her doubts.

Sunny tried not to appreciate how deftly and gently his

hands worked around the straps of her shoes, despite the size of his fingers. The man may have been crabby, but he was efficient, if nothing else. He finally stood, shoes in hand—forever endearing himself to her—and handed the slippers over to his daughter.

"What do you say to the princess?" he prodded.

The little girl hugged the slippers to her chest and looked up at her with big starstruck eyes. "Oh, thank you."

The boy folded his arms. "Do you have any pirate boots?"

Sunny chuckled but made a show of patting down her dress and looking around the ground. "You know what? I'm fresh out. Maybe next time."

"Well," the man said with a sigh. "Thanks to Princess Miranda here, I suppose we can all live happily ever after now. Thanks again," he called over his shoulder as he steered his children toward the exit.

Sunny waved to the children and watched them walk away. She turned around to go back to her post, but something in the father's sarcastic tone about happily-ever-afters gave her pause. The man obviously wasn't a believer in fairy tales. That was too bad. She'd still believe in them— even if she wasn't playing a princess. After everything that had happened in her life, fairy tales were all she had left. And the hope, *the dream* of something magical happening in her life was the only thing still keeping her going.

Chapter Two

Sunny shook off the sad vibe she'd gotten from the man and started weaving her way back to the photo post. Some of the children smiled and gawked as she passed them by. She waved and blew kisses, feeling in a much better mood since ditching those shoes—and just in time too. Her feet were still sore, but at least she'd avoided being maimed for life.

When she finally reached the photographer, his face looked pensive and—if she dared to say it—a little constipated. She hoped he hadn't had to deal with any angry parents while she was away. "Hey, sorry I'm late, Bud," she said, turning her back to him. "I hate to ask, but would you mind loosening up my cinches a bit?"

"Uh, well, okay." Bud tentatively retied the back of her dress. When he was done, she was able to take a big, satisfying, lung-filled breath.

She whirled around and kissed him on the cheek. "Thanks. You're the best."

Bud's cheeks colored. "Aw, now, Sunny. Don't be saying that. You're going make this harder than it already is."

"Make what harder?"

Bud paused, studying the gum- and popcorn-laden ground for a moment. "Mr. Twardski saw that you weren't at your post on time. Said he'd given you enough warnings. And, well, I'm sorry, Sunny, but it doesn't look good. He wants to see you in his office now."

Her breath caught for a few moments, apprehension washing over her. "He wants to see me? What do you think that means?"

But she had a feeling she already knew the answer.

Bud kept silent as he continued to study the ground. He obviously knew the answer too.

"Oh, no!" she cried. "But . . . but . . . there were two children—"

"Sunny," he said gently. "You're a nice girl. Look, if you need a job, I hear the Blowfish is going to be hiring a barmaid soon, since Cindy Townsend is going on maternity leave. I'm sure you'll be able to make decent tips, especially, well, looking the way you do."

Sunny blinked back the tears from her eyes. She was going to miss working with him. Miss working with the children. "Oh. Okay. Thanks, Bud. I'll check it out. You've been a good friend to me these past few weeks."

"Chin up, darlin'." He reached out and patted her head as she'd seen him do with upset children in the park. "I know you've had some tough times, but you don't need that old princess costume to have yourself that fairy-tale ending you've been talking about."

Sunny tried to summon up a smile for him but in the end

failed. She couldn't shake her worry. Bud didn't understand the amount of stress she'd been under trying to ward off the debt collectors *with* a job. She didn't know how long she could manage before she found another one.

Her dream of getting back on her feet and returning to school seemed so far off now, but she took Bud's hand and gave it a squeeze to reassure him she'd be okay, even if she didn't fully believe it herself. Then she turned toward Mr. Twardski's office. Deep in the back of her mind, Sunny knew it was silly to think she needed a princess costume to have her dreams come true, but it had been her best start.

"Okay, how about this one: *Have Viagra. Need woman. Nonsmoker preferred. Between ages of eighteen and fifty.* Ooh, and this one gives a P.O. box too. Bonus."

Sunny shot her friend Kim a withering glare. They'd been sitting in the Java Junkie all morning looking through want ads together. Apparently, they needed to take a break. Kim was starting to get punchy. "Oh, come on, Kim. Are you looking in the want-ad section or the personals section?"

Kim crossed her heart but laughed. "This is in the want ads. Honest. But I don't think it's so different from what that old coot Mr. Twardski wanted from you," she said, shaking her finger. "You know he wouldn't have fired you if you had given his son even half a glance."

She and Sunny exchanged horrified looks, then they both broke out laughing.

It felt so good to laugh. Too many months had gone by without it. Still smiling, Sunny rested her chin in her hand and scanned the paper again. "I don't know about that. Maybe I *was* late to my post a lot. But in all honesty, if Mr. Twardski had given me a costume I could have been a little more mobile in, I'm sure it would have made a difference."

Chuck, the postman, walked by their table and stopped when he heard Sunny's comment. "Yeah, but who wants to get their picture taken with a princess in a baggy old dress?" he asked, shooting her a good-natured wink. "And from what I'd seen on my delivery route, Sunny, you sure made one fine princess dressed the way you were. I'm sorry it didn't work out for you."

"Thanks, Chuck," Sunny said with a sigh. "Don't worry. I'm sure I'll find another job sooner or later." *Hopefully sooner.*

"That's the spirit!" Kim said, slapping her hands on the table. "Hey, did you go to the Blowfish Tavern like Bud mentioned?"

Sunny nodded. "Yeah, but the job's only Friday and Saturday nights. I won't earn enough with just that. I still need to find something during the week." She rubbed her temples, fighting off her rising anxiety at the lack of prospects. "What am I going to do, Kim? I need a real job, but without some sort of college degree, and the economy the way it is, it's slim pickings."

Kim laid a hand on her shoulder. "Don't get yourself all stressed out over this. We *will* find you a job. Things will work out, and if you need any money . . ."

Sunny's head sprang up. "*No.* Absolutely not. I will not take any money, especially from my best friend."

"Okay," Kim said gently. "I just want you to know, if you need it, you've got it."

"I know. I appreciate it," Sunny said as her gaze clouded with tears.

Kim's husband owned the coffee shop they were in, but Sunny knew things were tight all over, and they couldn't afford to be giving out handouts to every sob story like hers.

Sunny took a deep breath and reached out to lay a hand over Kim's. "I appreciate the offer, but I'll manage."

Somehow.

"Thanks a lot," Sam barked into his cell phone. "What do you mean, your delivery truck has a flat tire? Don't you people have backups in case of emergency? Wha—yes, actually, in my line of work a laptop delivery *is* considered an emergency. Okay. Fine. *Tomorrow.*" Sam shut off his cell phone with an unsatisfying beep. He tucked it into his pocket, then quickly reached out and grabbed his daughter's hood to keep her from wandering into the street.

"I'm hungry," Cole said, rubbing his tummy for effect.

Emma's eyes brightened at the mention of food. "Oooh, me too, Daddy! I'm tired of walking. We need a snack."

Sam scanned the avenue. He could barely enjoy the beautiful sunny day because his mind was on the work he still needed to get through today. But the kids were fighting a lot, so he knew if he was going to get anything done, he had to get them out of the house for a bit. Maybe there was a playground nearby. Then he could sit and call his partner, Mark, and see how things were progressing at the office without him. Sam had been bombarded with hundreds of e-mails this morning already. Apparently, there was a minor glitch with the partnership project they'd been working on. Not a good time to be without his computer. Hell, it wasn't a good time to be out of the office *period,* but once he found someone to take care of Emma and Cole, things would get a little easier.

He saw a sign with a big picture of a coffee cup on it and decided to take his kids in there to get a bite to eat and maybe grab a coffee for himself. "Okay, guys, how about a muffin or a piece of fruit or something?"

"May we have cookies?" Emma asked.

Sam's eyebrows drew together. "Cookies?"

"Yeah," Cole said, "Natasha would always give us cookies for a snack. Sometimes for breakfast too."

Oh, really? Cookies for breakfast? That was news to him. If he had known, he would have fired his nanny a lot earlier. It was bad enough she was always sneaking her boyfriends into the house when he had specifically asked her not to. But when he found out she was selling information about him and his children to *Star* magazine, he had her out the door. But what could he expect from the women in his life? Natasha the Nanny was now another name added to the list of Women Who Had Used Him.

Unfortunately, at the top of that list was his very own mother.

"No cookies," Sam scolded, "but we'll see if we can get you guys something healthy to eat." Sam opened the door and led them inside the coffeehouse. As soon as he stepped in, his nose was hit hard with the aroma of fresh-brewed coffee and cinnamon. His stomach gurgled, and he remembered that, although he'd fed his kids, he'd skipped breakfast himself.

The children ran up to the counter to look at the huge display of pastries. Sam looked around for an open table and to get a feel for the place, but a head of blond hair immediately caught his eye. His whole body tensed.

It was the princess—er, *woman*—from the amusement park. He was sure of it. He could only see part of her profile, but he would recognize that shade of platinum anywhere. Two days had gone by since he'd seen her, but something about their meeting had stuck in his mind, and he hadn't been able to block it out. She had looked so . . . well, sweaty for one thing, but he had also seen an air of vulnerability in her eyes that had unnerved him; it had put him on high alert. He had fallen for that sad, sexy look before. Women always used that method when they wanted something from him. Beautiful women like that didn't just materialize out of nowhere saying they had found your missing children out of the goodness of their hearts. Fat chance. She wanted something. In fact, he was surprised the "princess" hadn't asked him for some kind of reward for keeping his children safe.

His son tugged on the end of his shirt to grab his attention. "Emma and I want chocolate donuts. Frosted, with sprinkles."

Sam tore his gaze away from the blond woman—hoping she wouldn't see them—and smiled down at his children. "No donuts today," he said, keeping his voice low.

"May we get brownies?" Cole asked.

Sam shook his head. "How about a raisin bran muffin?"

Emma's little nose wrinkled. "Eww. But I don't like *waisins,* Daddy."

"Well, I personally *love* raisins," said a familiar feminine voice.

Sam tensed. He didn't have to look to know who had said those words. He let out a quiet sigh. It was silly to think the blond wouldn't recognize them or try to talk to them again. She obviously was after something.

"*Pwincess Miwanda!*" Emma squealed. "Don't worry, we still have your slippers."

"Yeah," Cole said, "we're taking good care of them."

The woman smiled sweetly at his children—a little too sweetly—almost as if a glimmer of sunshine had suddenly brightened up their little corner of the coffee shop. *Oh, brother.* He folded his arms and resisted the urge to scoff at his own analogy.

Amusement danced in the woman's eyes. "I'm so glad to hear that. I knew I could trust you two with my shoes." She winked and then looked up at Sam. "Hi."

Sam stared at her for a few seconds, suddenly feeling sucker punched. Okay. He had to give her some credit. She was one heck of a natural beauty. Without all that caked-on Princess Miranda makeup, she looked younger today, more vibrant. Sexier.

He swallowed hard, angry at the way his thoughts were double-crossing him. "Uh, hello," he finally mumbled with a frown.

"I saw you walk in, so I thought I'd come over and say hi." She bit her lip and glanced over her shoulder, looking as if she suddenly regretted that move.

Smart woman. She was obviously getting the hint from his expression that she wasn't wanted here.

"Oh, no! Where is your crown and dress?" Emma asked, pointing to Sunny's green T-shirt and white shorts. Sam automatically dropped his gaze and was greeted by the sight of a long, lightly tanned pair of legs. *Nice,* he thought. Then he cleared his throat and looked up. Getting sidetracked by a pair of legs wasn't like him. He must be spending way too much time in front of a computer screen lately.

"Well, I have to confess. My name isn't really Princess Miranda. Um, at least not anymore. My name is Sunny," she said, blushing.

24   *Jennifer Shirk*

"I knew it!" Cole exclaimed, elbowing Sam. "I told you she was a fake princess."

Sunny drew herself up into a regal posture. "Hey, I'm not a fake. You don't need to have a title or crown to be royalty. I believe there is a little bit of princess inside every woman—or girl, for that matter," she said, looking down at Emma.

Emma got a gleam in her eye and looked up at Sunny as though she were the best thing since birthday-cake-flavored ice cream. "You mean *I'm* a *pwincess* too?" she asked in wonder.

"Why, of course," Sunny said with an elegant nod.

Sam inwardly rolled his eyes, fighting the urge to smirk, as well. Was this woman for real? "Okay, let me guess," he said, playing along with the woman's over-the-top act. "Sunny is just a nickname, and your real name is . . . Little Miss Sunshine."

Sunny frowned, and the light that had been shining through those pale blue green eyes of hers dimmed, making him feel like a first-class heel. *Well, there you go.* Leave it to him to darken a mood. He was obviously out of practice talking with women outside of work. But since his divorce three years ago, he'd worked hard to steer clear of romantic involvements.

Sunny turned away, chuckling at something Emma said, and the light was back in her eyes. Sam was glad he hadn't completely snuffed it out. The glow of her smile was nice, almost as if it were full of hope.

A smile full of hope?

Hope? He almost laughed out loud at such a romantic thought. What the heck was going on with him? This woman had probably figured out who he was and *hoped* he'd give her a diamond ring—or at least a diamond bracelet. Yeah, Sam knew better than to trust a pretty smile like that again.

"Um, no," Sunny said. "My real name is Sunnyva."

"*Sunnyva?*" he repeated.

She shrugged a delicate shoulder. "You can blame my Scandinavian grandmother for that one. She was big on family heritage. Everyone just calls me Sunny, though."

No, not him. He wouldn't be calling her anything. In fact, he wanted to get away from her. Fast. The woman was trying to charm him, and even though he knew better, it was actually working. Maybe he could convince his kids to get their muffins to go so he could make a clean escape before she shot him any more of her *hopeful* smiles.

His cell phone went off then. Great. Perfect timing, as usual. He shrugged apologetically and plucked it out of his pocket, glancing at the number. It was his secretary, which meant it was important. With the looming deadline on his possible merger with Yahoo! he had no choice but to take the call. He looked at his children, waiting anxiously to be fed, and felt like a heel all over again. "Uh . . . look, guys, I really need to take this. No fooling. It'll just take a minute, though."

Emma and Cole made faces and moaned. "You always say it'll take a minute, and it never does," Cole complained. "It always takes all day."

"I can order them something to eat for you," Sunny offered. "Go ahead and take your call. I'm not going anywhere anytime soon."

Sam was afraid of that, but he shot Sunny a grateful smile anyway as he handed her a twenty-dollar bill. Then he turned away and found a quiet corner to take his call. He really hoped this woman didn't have any ulterior motive in helping out, but he would take her help nonetheless. Maybe Sunny wasn't a true princess, but right now, she was one heck of a royal lifesaver.

Sunny ordered the children two whole wheat blueberry muffins and two chocolate milks and brought them over to the table where she and Kim were sitting.

Kim glanced up from the paper when she heard them approach. "Uh, you were supposed to come back with two cappuccinos, not two children," she said with a wink. "So who do we have here?"

"This is Emma," Sunny said, placing her hand on the girl's strawberry red hair. "And this is Cole," she said, gesturing to the boy. "Their dad is over there taking an important phone call."

Kim craned her neck to see the man in question. She raised her eyebrows and shot her a look Sunny knew well—Kim thought the dad was a superhunk. Sunny wasn't going to disagree with her on that one, but the last thing she needed was to get involved with anyone, let alone a married father of twins, while she was still trying to get her life in order.

Sunny chuckled when Kim continued to eye the man up. "It's not like that," she assured her friend. "These are the kids I told you about from the boardwalk."

"Oh, you mean the ones who got you fired?"

Cole looked up from his muffin and frowned. "What's *fired* mean?"

Sunny scowled at Kim for opening her big mouth in front of them, then turned to Cole. "Um, it means—"

"You should ask your father," Kim said with a smirk.

Cole nodded and went back to shoveling more muffin into his mouth.

Kim aimed critical eyes at Sunny as she leaned in and lowered her voice. "So, you *find* his children, and now you're *watching* them too?" she asked sharply. "Honestly, Sunny, you need to grow a backbone and say no for once."

"Well, I was standing there, and he seemed to need help and . . ." Sunny shrugged feebly. Oh, what did Kim know? She had a backbone. Sort of. It just so happened to be a nice one. She wasn't Mother Teresa or anything, but if she saw someone or something that needed help, she wasn't one to turn away. Her grandmother had instilled in her values like that, always reminding Sunny that good deeds done bring good fortune back. Sunny honestly believed those words.

It was just that *her* good fortune was taking its time in arriving. That's all.

Kim shook her head. "You're a saint—you know that, right? So what's the busy-important-call-taker's name?"

Name?

Sunny's eyes widened. Hmm . . . funny how he'd never gotten around to giving her his name. Not that she'd asked him for it.

"Oh, for goodness' sake. I don't believe you," Kim admonished. "You're watching his kids, and you don't even know his name?" She turned to his children. "Hey, guys, what's your daddy's name?"

"Sam," they said with their mouths full.

Kim shot Sunny a smug look. "See how hard that was?" She turned back to the children, resting her elbows on the table. "So, uh, what does your daddy do for a living?"

"Kim!" Sunny cried. "I don't think we should pry."

"He plays on computers a lot," Cole answered.

"Ah, a techno geek," Kim confirmed, and Sunny shot her a warning look.

Cole licked his thumb and continued. "He's super busy all the time. That's why we need a new nanny."

"Nanny?" Sunny asked, her interest piqued. Their father was going to hire a nanny. She could be a nanny. She *thought* she could, anyway. Children seemed to like her. Maybe this was the good fortune she'd been waiting for to arrive.

Emma took her straw out of her milk and began chewing on the end. "Yeah, our last nanny couldn't move here with us. She was mad. Natasha looked like this." Sunny choked on a laugh as Emma scrunched up her face and proceeded to do a pretty good imitation of one angry nanny.

Sunny drummed her fingers on the table, trying to come up with a way to delicately ask the next question. "Um, so, where's your mommy?"

Kim cocked an eyebrow. "Gee, I thought you didn't want to pry."

"Oh, shush," she said, waving the comment away.

Cole's face grew long. "Mommy's not on this planet anymore. Daddy said the angels had to take her. We'll get to see her again someday, though."

Kim and Sunny exchanged sympathetic looks. Sunny wanted to ask the children a few more questions— particularly pertaining to what, exactly, their nanny did to get fired—but at that moment Sam appeared at the table.

Sam's shoulders sagged once he glanced at the empty wrappers and muffins crumbs on the table. "I, uh, guess I took a little longer than a minute."

"See? It always takes forever, Daddy," Emma said. "We told you."

Sam ran a hand through his rich, dark hair and gave them a half smile. "Yeah, I'm sorry about that."

"No problem . . . *Sam*," Sunny said, emphasizing his name and trying it out for size on her tongue. She decided she liked it. And she liked him too—much more so now that she knew he had the power to give her a job—despite his reserved manner. *Sam* was such a simple, no-nonsense name. Much like the man himself appeared to be. She could work for someone like him. He seemed to really need her help too.

Sam smiled sheepishly. "Oh, right. I guess you figured that much out." He held out his hand to make their introduction official. "Sam Calloway."

"Sunny Fletcher. And this is my friend Kim O'Connor."

He nodded. "Nice to officially meet you both."

"Sam Calloway?" Kim asked. "Are you renting the bay house on Walnut Street?"

Sam's expression became wary. "Yes, I am. Why?"

"Oh, well, then we're going to be neighbors. For the summer, at least. I live down the street. On the *non*water side," she quipped.

Sunny clasped her hands together, hoping to come up with another topic so she could keep him around a little longer and perhaps ease into the topic of the nanny position without looking desperate. Less desperate than she was, anyway.

"Daddy, what's *fired* mean?"

Sunny cringed. Oh, no. This was not *easing into* the topic.

Sam glanced at his son with a confused expression. "Fired?"

"Yeah," Cole said, bobbing his head. "We fired Sunny."

Sunny covered her face with her hands. She wanted to

slither under the table and die. Right *after* she killed Kim for letting that information slip out in front of the children.

"What does he mean?" Sam asked.

Sunny peeked at Sam through her fingers. Concerned gray eyes peered back. Suddenly she had a hard time breathing, and her cheeks felt like a four-alarm fire was going to break out on them at any moment. "Oh. Well, I was sort of fired from my princess job. But it wasn't their fault."

"That's right," Kim interjected. "It's not their fault. But maybe if their father had kept a better eye on his kids, they wouldn't have gotten lost in the first place."

Sunny shot her friend another warning look, then spoke between clenched teeth. "I'm sure what Kim means to say is that *no one* is to blame. It's just that when I stopped to help Emma and Cole, I was late for my post." *Again.* But she decided not to mention the multiple-lateness part to a possible new employer.

"Oh. That's unfortunate. I'm very sorry that happened." Sam's words were polite but were delivered with hard eyes and a mouth drawn in a tight line, hardly making him look concerned or even sorry she'd lost her job. He quickly checked his watch. "I need to get going."

Kim kicked her under the table, signaling her to say something about the nanny position before he disappeared.

"Ow!" Sunny scowled at Kim. Rubbing her shin, she turned to Sam. "Uh, look, I was wondering, since I need a job now, and you're, well . . ."

A dawning of realization sparked in Sam's eyes, and his expression grew several degrees colder. "Ah, I see what this is all about. Now I know why you were so eager to help me. I'm sorry, but my company isn't hiring at the moment. Of course, you're welcome to send in your resume for us to have on file."

Resume? Company? She didn't even know he had a company to send a resume to. "Um, no, actually, I was more interested in the, uh, *nanny* position."

Sam blinked, then threw his head back and laughed. "You want me to hire you as a nanny?"

Emma stopped blowing bubbles in her milk and looked up with wide, excited eyes. "Sunny's going to be our new nanny?"

"Oh, cool!" Cole exclaimed. "You're not mean like Natasha was, and you're not old like that Mrs. Ferguson. Mrs. Ferguson was always putting things where they didn't belong, and she couldn't see so good."

Sam gave him a stern look. "Hey, that's not nice to say, Cole."

"Sorry. But if she was a knight, she would be Mrs. Forgets-a-lot."

Sunny banked down a bubble of laughter.

"Well, it doesn't matter how Mrs. Ferguson was, because Sunny is *not* going to be your new nanny," Sam firmly told them.

Any lingering laughter Sunny might have had died on the spot. "Oh, but I do have references!" she cried. "I've done a little babysitting on the side for years. I can be at your house at whatever time you want, except Friday and Saturday nights. And . . . and . . . I—I can even cook. Sometimes."

"*Sometimes?*" he asked.

She shrugged guiltily. "Well, it's usually hit-or-miss. I do make very good peanut butter and jelly sandwiches, and last year at the County Fall Festival I took first place for my double chocolate chip brownies."

Sam let out an audible sigh. If Sunny were a betting woman, she'd wager he didn't seem too impressed with those credentials. "Look, miss, I prefer using an agency and going through all the proper channels. No offense. And I need someone willing to put in at least fifty hours a week."

Sunny almost pinched herself when she heard *fifty hours a week*. That would pull in a lot of money. She obviously wasn't doing a great job selling herself, though. Sam was already back to calling her *miss* instead of Sunny. She needed this job. But what else could she say? She finally looked to Kim for help.

Kim took the cue and stood, taking Sam by the arm and leading him out of earshot of the children. "Well, just so you know," she said in a hushed tone, "this is a small town. There's no agency here, and from what your children said, I'm not so sure you've had the greatest luck with that. So, you should at least consider Sunny. It's really simple when you think about it. You need a nanny, and she needs a job. Anyone in town will vouch for her. And she did care enough about your children to leave her princess post. Heck, if you'd use your eyes, you can see for yourself that she's great with your kids."

Sam rolled his eyes, then let his gaze fall to his children. Emma had already climbed up onto Sunny's lap, running her little fingers through Sunny's straight blond hair. Cole looked at his father, then clasped his hands in prayer position. Sunny said a silent prayer too. She held her breath and waited.

Sam walked back toward them with a resigned look. His cell phone went off again, but he ignored it this time. Pinching the bridge of his nose, he finally muttered, "Fine."

"Yay!" the kids shouted, giggling and dancing around the table.

The breath Sunny had been holding rushed out of her lungs. She almost thought she'd misheard him. "You mean it? You'll really hire me?"

"Yeah, but let's not get carried away. It'll just be temporary. Let's see how the week goes first."

Sunny high-fived Kim, then jumped out of her chair. She was so happy, she almost threw her arms around Sam and kissed him. Fortunately, Sam's disapproving scowl kept her firmly rooted to the two-foot distance between them. He didn't have much confidence in her, but that was okay. She had more than enough for both of them.

"Oh, you won't be sorry," she assured him. "I'll be the best nanny slash brownie maker slash ex-princess you've ever had. I guarantee, after this week, you'll be so pleased, you won't ever want to let me go."

Sam folded his arms and smirked. "Yeah, well, we'll see about that."

Chapter Three

Sunny was going to be late.

That was bad enough, but it also wasn't the kind of impression she wanted to convey to someone like Sam Calloway on her first day of work. He didn't need any excuse to fire her. The man had barely wanted to hire her as his children's nanny in the first place. Luckily, she'd been able to convince him that she'd do a great job. Now she only had to prove it. She didn't want to lose this job before she had even begun it, but if she was going to show up late for work, at least she had a darn good excuse: Oats, her golden retriever, wouldn't eat.

Sunny bent down, taking her dog's face into her hands, and looked lovingly into her eyes. "What's the matter, girl? You love this stuff. It has real chicken and liver in it. Yum, yum, yum."

Oats dropped down on her tummy and laid her chin on the floor.

"Uh-uh. Don't do this to Mommy. Not today. You *have* to eat. I know I've been leaving you alone a lot, but you just have to suck it up and be a big girl—er, dog."

Oats let out a low moan.

Sunny sighed and glanced at the time again. If she didn't leave now, there would be no *going* to be late. She *would be* late for sure.

"Okay. Fine," she said, coming up with the only viable solution. "You're going to have to come with me, then."

Oats didn't lift her head, but her tail thumped up and down on the floor. Sunny smiled. The dog obviously liked the idea of coming along with her. Maybe Sunny was babying her, but she couldn't help it. Oats was the only family she had left now.

When she had first seen Oats at the animal shelter, it was love at first limp. Someone had found the dog hurt on the side of a road and brought her into the shelter, where Sunny volunteered the little free time she had. The veterinarian on duty had diagnosed one of the dog's legs with a fracture and had put a splint on it. Sunny had felt so sorry for the shaggy dog, she'd decided to adopt her right then and there and nurse her back to health herself. It had turned out to be the best decision she'd ever made, because Oats was a wonderful source of companionship to her after her grandma died.

Sunny grabbed her purse and filled it with biscuits, bones, and a few rubber toys. She glanced back at Oats, who was now on her feet with her face in her food bowl.

Hmm. She was probably faking the whole sad and sickly act. But Sunny would take her to work anyway. She couldn't take the chance in case there really was something wrong with her dog.

Being a family man, Sam, she was sure, would understand.

Sam checked his watch. Sunny still had five more minutes to get there, but he was anxious.

He needed to call his VP of engineering operations, and he couldn't do that until he knew his children were settled and attended to. He hoped this situation with Sunny worked out and he hadn't made a mistake in hiring her. Something about the woman put him on edge. Not her looks, as physically appealing as she was. No, he could handle a pretty face just fine. What he couldn't handle was someone trying to use him or his children. But he needed the help right now, and he felt a small pang of guilt for having had a hand in getting her fired from her princess job. All of Sunny's references had checked out, which satisfied his safety concerns, and enough people in town seemed to know and like her. He would just have to keep a close eye on her and make sure that sweet act was legit. He refused to take any chances where his kids were concerned.

The doorbell rang, breaking him from his thoughts, and he rushed over to answer it. When he swung open the door and saw her standing there with a golden retriever at her feet, he should have been surprised. But somehow he wasn't. Before Sam had hired Sunny, he already had an odd sense there wasn't anything predictable or mundane about this woman.

"You've got to be kidding," he said in greeting to Sunny. "Who in their right mind brings their dog to work without clearing it with their employer?" He looked down at her large canine sidekick again and folded his arms, blocking their entrance. There was no way he wanted a dog with a tail that looked as though it could take out a small city coming into his home and knocking over any of his computer equipment.

"I can explain," she said quickly.

"Oh, naturally," he said, leaning against the door frame. "By all means, please do."

Sunny bit her lip, tucking little blond pieces of hair that had fallen out of her ponytail behind her ears. "Well, uh, under normal circumstances I would never even *think* about bringing my dog to any job I had—assuming I still have a job after this—but I didn't want to be late, so I had to make a split-second decision. Oats was acting funny this morning, and I didn't want to take a chance that she could be sick."

He threw his hands up in the air. "Oh, great, so you brought a *sick* dog here?"

"Well"—she visibly swallowed hard, and he fought the urge to smile at the cute little lines of worry etched between her eyebrows—"um, yeah. If it makes you feel better, I think Oatsie here is already on the mend," she said, giving the dog a few quick pats on her head.

The dog gave a large *woof* and jumped up, placing her two big front paws on Sam's chest. Sam's lips thinned as he examined Oats. The dog didn't look sick to him—but it could sure use a breath mint and maybe a bath.

"Ooops. Sorry. Bad girl," Sunny scolded as she tugged on the dog's collar. "Get down."

The children ran to the door when they heard the dog bark and squealed with delight when they saw the hairy animal. *Great.* It looked like old Oats was here for the duration. Sam's only hope was that the dog was at least housebroken.

Sunny beamed at the children's response to her pet. "This is my dog, Oats," she told them. "She loves it when you scratch under her tummy like this." Sunny's hand traveled to the dog's stomach, and Oats automatically flipped onto her back with her legs in the air, sending Sam's kids into hysterical giggles.

Sunny let the children take over scratching Oats and slowly blinked her blue eyes up at Sam, giving him one of her sweet smiles. She looked so childlike herself, he couldn't help but smile back. She was just so darn . . . likeable. Then he realized what she was doing to him, and he frowned. The woman didn't have to say a word, and he was already succumbing to her charm.

And he didn't like it one bit.

"Is it all right if my dog stays?" she asked.

"Yes, the dog can stay," he grumbled.

Sunny clasped her hands together and beamed. "Oh, thank you, Sam—er, Mr. Cal—er—"

"Just call me Sam," he said dryly. "Since your dog has just been temporarily adopted by my children, I think we're past any employer-employee formalities now."

Emma looked up from petting Oats. "And we can call you Sunny, right, Sunny? Because I know that's your name. It's kind of funny, though."

"Emma," her father admonished.

Sunny laughed. "It's okay. You're right, Emma. It is unusual, but I like to think of it as . . . *special* also."

Special?

Sam cocked his head as he studied Sunny. Almost all of her hair had escaped out of her ponytail now. She wore a baggy pink sweatshirt and had on the kind of drawstring plaid pants that would've set Bozo the Clown's heart pitter-pattering with envy. Her yellow tennis shoes were covered with dog hair.

Yeah, *special* was one word for her.

Emma knelt again and hugged the dog. "Oh, I want to marry Oats," she announced.

"You can't marry Oats, because I'm going to marry her," Cole told his sister.

Sam finally broke out in a laugh. The situation was all

too ridiculous. But he enjoyed seeing his children so enthused and happy. Actually, it had been a long time since he'd felt this lighthearted himself. It was a strange sensation. "You're *both* too young to get married, so forget it," he said, trying for a straight face. "Now, let's get Sunny and Oats into the house so Daddy can get some work done."

Work . . .

Holy crap. He'd gotten so caught up in Sunny and her dog, he'd forgotten about his conference call and the pile of work he had waiting. How much time had he just wasted?

Sam quickly stepped back to allow Sunny entrance, and as she passed him, he caught a whiff of her shampoo. The fresh and flowery scent reflected her personality so well. Just like her name: Sunny. The woman seemed to be chock-full of rainbows and sunshine—a regular living, breathing Disney princess character. Probably the kind of character who had never known any heartache in her life. He doubted she'd be so open and chipper if she had. His mood suddenly grew a little resentful as a result.

"I need to get to work now," he said, sounding a little gruffer than he'd intended. "Don't let the kids watch too much TV, and there's plenty of food to fix for whatever they want for lunch. I left a list of do's and don'ts on the counter. Don't worry about making dinner tonight. I plan on ordering out."

Sunny bent down to take off Oats' leash. Emma and Cole were already arguing about who was going to get to throw a ball to her first. "What about *your* lunch?" she asked, pointing those clear blue eyes at him again.

The question threw him off guard. None of the other nannies he'd hired had ever worried if he ate or not. "If I'm hungry, I'll come down and grab something myself. Just take care of the kids. And your dog," he added.

She cocked her head, giving him a look that was all wide-eyed with concern. "But you have to eat."

"Yeah, Daddy," Emma said, her arms still wrapped around Oats' neck. "You need your *stwength*."

"I'll be fine." He walked over and pressed a kiss onto his daughter's head. "If you need anything," he told Sunny over his shoulder, "try to find it on your own first. But if you get desperate, I'll be in my office upstairs. Both of you, be good for Sunny."

"We will," his children answered.

Sunny carefully cut the crusts off two peanut butter—no jelly—sandwiches as the kids played fetch with Oats. She quickly found out that Emma and Cole were a handful. But they were a lot of fun too. Someday she hoped to have children of her own. Spending time with them filled an emptiness she didn't even realize was inside her, or maybe she was just lonely since Mom-mom's passing. Either way, she really liked Emma and Cole, and she liked this job.

Unfortunately, the jury was still out on her boss.

Thinking of Sam, Sunny glanced at the far end of the hall. His office door remained closed. Sam had been locked in there all morning. She hadn't even seen him come out to use the bathroom yet. She bit her lip. Maybe she should go in and check on him.

"No, Sunny," she told herself, "you're the children's nanny. You're not *his* nanny. He made that perfectly clear." But then she glanced at the door again.

Was he all right? What if he was dead? What if he'd had a heart attack or stroke and was slumped over his desk right this very minute? If she checked on him now, there would still be time to call 911. Possibly even save his life.

That did it. There was no sense in coming up with any more lame excuses. She rinsed her hands, then wiped them on her pants. She was going to satisfy her curiosity and check on him, and that was that. Besides, no matter what he had told her, he still needed to eat.

Sunny walked over to the patio doors and called Emma and Cole in for lunch. The kids and Oats automatically ran in. After pouring them each a glass of milk, she picked up the chicken salad sandwich she'd made for herself and decided to deliver it to Sam. "Stay here, guys. I'm going to go give this to your Dad. If you eat your whole sandwich and drink all your milk, I have something special we could do this afternoon," she added.

Cole started shoving the sandwich into his mouth. "Look, Sunny, I'm almost done," he mumbled.

Sunny frowned. "It's not a race, Cole. Besides, if you choke to death, you won't be around to do what I have planned."

Cole's eyes widened, and he began taking smaller bites.

"Good," she said with a chuckle. "Now, I'll be right back."

Sunny kicked off her sneakers and treaded softly up the steps to Sam's office door in her bare feet, not wanting to make any unnecessary noise. Leaning her ear against the wood paneling, she heard talking. *Good sign,* she thought. He wasn't dead. And he was probably hungry. Balancing the plate in one hand, she lightly knocked with her other. Some kind of grunt answered her. She decided to take that as "come in" and opened the door.

Sam was sitting hunched over his desk. He wore a Bluetooth headset, talking into the little speaker as he looked through papers with one hand and wrote down notes with the other. He never looked up when she walked in.

Sunny took the opportunity to glance around his office a bit as she and her sandwich made their way to his desk. Sam had an L-shaped cherrywood desk set right in front of the windows, overlooking his bayside backyard. However, the blinds were drawn closed, which she thought was odd. Two metal bookcases armed with computer reference material and binders stood side by side along one of the walls. He hadn't hung up any pictures yet, nor were there any on his desk. There were no plants or any other sign of life except the fax machine on the floor behind him, buzzing and spitting out papers as he talked.

If he hadn't looked up at her at that very moment, she would have made a face. What a dismal environment to work in. He might as well have been working in a cave.

She schooled her feelings on how he conducted his business and summoned up a cheery smile. "I thought you could use a break," she whispered, trying not to disrupt his phone call.

Sam squinted at her. She wasn't sure if he hadn't heard her or if he hadn't heard of a break before. As she looked around the room at the piles of folders and books on the floor, she was beginning to believe the latter.

She pointed to the desk. "I can leave it here."

Sam held up a finger and spun around in his chair to lift out the papers from the fax. "Yeah, I got them," he said into the speaker. "Let me look them over, and I'll give you a call back." He whipped off his headset and turned back around. "What is it?"

Sunny blinked. Sam actually sounded as if he were annoyed. *Gee whiz, you try to make sure your employer isn't dead and bring him some sustenance, and that's the thanks you get.* "I brought you a sandwich," she said, indicating the plate.

"I don't want any food."

"Well, I know, but, um, it's lunchtime," she answered lamely. "I thought you might be hungry."

Sam glanced at his watch. "Is it? I didn't realize it was so late. But I can't take lunch right now," he said, ignoring her again and sorting through his faxed papers. "Take it away."

Sunny set a hand on her hip. Her patience was wearing thin. "I'm not asking you to *take lunch.* I'm just giving you a sandwich to eat while you work." *My sandwich to eat while you work,* she wanted to add. "Surely you can spare two seconds to take a bite. Emma and Cole are even taking a break from playing with Oats."

She finally had Sam's attention at the mere mention of his children's names. "Is there a problem with the kids?" he asked.

"No. No problem." She sighed. "I told you. They're eating lunch now. Like *you* should be eating lunch."

He sat back, and his gaze locked on hers. Sam was such a handsome man—even when he looked cross. It was a shame his personality didn't match his looks. He was so testy. She'd have to be blind not to see that he didn't appreciate being lectured. She would make a mental note of that one for future reference.

The silence between them dragged on. The intensity of his stare made her feel as if she were on a stage. She couldn't even begin to figure out what he must be thinking, but she hoped it wouldn't lead to the words, *You're fired.* Her heart began to hammer in her chest. Why couldn't she control her

mouth? She didn't know why she'd made such a fuss about
his not eating anyway. Now that Mom-mom wasn't around,
Sunny was beginning to sound just like her. Not that she
considered that a bad thing, really.

Sam finally reached for the plate and slowly made a show
of lifting and taking a bite of his sandwich. "Happy?" he
asked with his mouth full.

Her shoulders relaxed, and she was able to let out a long,
slow breath. "Yes, very happy. Well, I guess my work here
for the nutrition council is done," she said with a grin and a
mock salute.

Sam didn't return her grin. He picked up his headset,
placed it back around his head, and started punching in a
phone number. She mentally rolled her eyes. He sure wasn't
the chitchat type. But before she lectured him on that, too,
she took her cue to leave and made a beeline for the door.

"Sunny," he called as she reached the doorknob.

She tensed at the authoritative command in his tone, then
tentatively turned around. "Yes?"

"Thank you." This time he did give her a smile. A real
smile. One that made him look so breathtakingly handsome,
her heart almost stopped beating at that very moment.

She placed her hand limply on her chest and tried to swal-
low, but her mouth suddenly went dry. "Uh, yeah, thanks,"
she said, a little dazed at her reaction to him.

His eyes crinkled in a further appealing manner, and her
heart turned over in response. "I think your response is
supposed to be 'You're welcome.'"

"Huh? Oh, right." She blinked and mentally kicked herself.
*Get a grip, Sunny. The man is just thankful for a sandwich.
Try not to drool all over him, for goodness' sake.* Without

another word, she turned around and hurried out of his office, closing the door behind her with a soft click.

Slumped up against the other side of the door, she closed her eyes and tried to collect her wits. She didn't know what had just happened back there, but it concerned her. Was she actually attracted to her boss? No. She couldn't be. Sam might be a caring father, but he was such a . . . such a . . . He was just plain wrong—wrong man, wrong time, wrong *everything*. Sam didn't fit the fairy-tale mold Mom-mom had placed in her mind at all. Besides, she couldn't lust after her employer. Leave it to her to almost mess up a good thing when she had one. She needed this job—not a boyfriend.

She hoped that zing of attraction was just a fluke. If she wanted to keep this job, she'd have to remember to keep her feelings in check the next time they interacted. That shouldn't pose a problem. Although Sam Calloway was quite handsome, that was all he had going for him. One thing she could be sure of was that Sam was no Prince Charming.

Sam stood and stretched, trying to work out the kinks in his back. He'd been poring over contracts for the last nine hours straight. There was still more work to be done, but he'd give it a rest for now. Once the kids went to bed for the night, he would go back and do a little more.

He glanced at the empty plate Sunny had used for his lunch and smiled. She was something else, making sure he didn't skip a meal—like a little mother hen. A *bossy* mother hen. But it was kind of sweet, almost as if she really cared about his welfare. It'd been a long time since he'd felt anything remotely like that from a woman. He wondered if he had misjudged her.

Laughter outside caught his attention. Sam stood and walked over to the window. He drew back the blinds and peered down. The day must have warmed up, because Sunny had removed her sweatshirt, leaving her with just a tiny white tank top. He couldn't help but admire her willowy body, despite the baggy pants that still hid most it. He frowned and tore his gaze away, trying to concentrate on his kids instead. Sunny was leading them in a game of Red Light, Green Light. Cole was about to tag her but lost his balance and tumbled at her feet. Emma then tagged Sunny and whooped with joy at this small victory over her brother.

Despite his initial reservations over hiring Sunny—and his body's sudden inclination to notice how attractive she was—he was glad she was here with them. Since meeting her, he'd never seen his children so happy. They hadn't been this happy even when their mother was alive. Sam gazed at Sunny again as his thoughts drifted to his ex-wife. Would Kate have played with their kids like that if she were alive today? Probably not. A stab of sadness struck his heart. Kate didn't even want to have the twins in the first place. She was afraid a pregnancy might end her modeling career too early. But in the end he had talked her into becoming a mom. However, their relationship was never the same after that.

Sunny suddenly looked up and caught him staring at her like a fool. She waved happily at him, directing Emma and Cole's attention up toward the window to where he was standing. Sam numbly lifted his hand, still a little depressed over the circumstances in his life, but then laughed when Emma started dancing goofily and showing off for him.

His kids were everything to him now. And as soon as his work situation slowed down, he vowed to spend much more time with them.

His phone rang, and he frowned. He reluctantly stepped away from the window and answered it.

"Hi, darling," his mother cooed on the other end.

Sam gritted his teeth. Speak of the *other* depressing woman in his life. But he banked down his sour mood and tried to sound at the very least . . . pleasant. "Hi, Mom. What's going on?"

"What's going on? I'll tell you what's going on. My son has taken my only two grandchildren and hidden them away in some godforsaken little town in the country. How am I supposed to visit them? There's nothing around there. Couldn't you have at least considered the Hamptons?"

Oh, of course, what was I thinking? he thought cynically. Perhaps Beverly Hills would have been better? Leave it to his mom to worry more about the town and what there was for her to do in it rather than simply visiting because she wanted to see Emma and Cole.

"It's a nice town, Mom. Emma and Cole need some quiet country. It's been too hectic for them in the city. I want them to take it easy a bit before school starts again. You know, climb a tree."

"Climb a tree?" His mother sounded outraged. "There are trees in Central Park."

He sighed and turned to look out the window again. Cole and Emma were taking turns pushing Sunny on a swing now. His mood strangely lifted, and he found he could smile. "No, Mom. It's not just that. Look, is there another reason for this call?"

His mother sniffed. "Well, I *am* your mother. I didn't know I needed a reason. You never even call me. I could be lying dead in my apartment, and you'd never know for weeks."

Sam rolled his eyes at his mother's dramatic tactics. The

woman was sixty and as healthy as a horse. Heck, he'd lay odds she'd outlive him. "With the kind of social life you have, Mom, one of your friends would find you within ten seconds, I'm sure. I wouldn't worry if I were you."

"Well, you never know. You should call more anyway. But that's not the reason I wanted to talk to you."

Here it comes, he thought. It never failed. She wanted something.

"I've been thinking, Sam, since you're not using your town house this summer, I could maybe watch it for you."

"You mean like house-sit?"

"Why, yes. Exactly. I could house-sit for you, uh, with a few of my lady friends from the yacht club. They've always wanted to stay in New York City and catch a show. I thought it would be fun for us for at least a week or so."

"Fine," he said, closing his eyes and wishing the conversation was already over. "Whatever you want to do is fine. We won't be back until a few weeks before the school year starts, so whenever you want to go there is fine. I'll call security and let them know you'll be coming."

"Oh, thank you. That's great. You're such a good boy. I can't wait to tell my friends. Give Emma and Cole my love. Ciao." The other end of the line clicked off before he could respond.

Sam shook his head as he put the phone back into his pocket. It amazed him how he was always labeled *a good boy* when his mom got her own way. Did his mother ever call when she didn't want something? He couldn't remember the last time she had. That was a telltale sign. Not that it mattered. His heart was frozen now when it came to women in his life anyway. His ex-wife had solidified that.

Sam walked over to the window again and drew the

blinds, determined not to give his mother or his new nanny another thought. He was on his own now—just him and his children.

And he preferred it stay that way.

Chapter Four

Helping out in the town's only no-kill animal shelter was one of the things Sunny looked forward to in the week. Her life was already full balancing two jobs: nanny to Sam's children and waitressing at the Blowfish Tavern. The position at the tavern involved weekend nights, so she was relieved she could still volunteer her time at the shelter on Saturday mornings. She even convinced Kim to come and help out.

Financially, things were still tight, since she hadn't collected a paycheck yet for either job. She hoped Sam hadn't forgotten the salary he'd promised her. She was counting on that exact amount so she could pay her bills and have just enough left over to save for college—something she'd promised Mom-mom she'd go back to do.

Sunny rolled up her sleeves, about to refill the hamsters' water bottle, when Kim walked in and began pressing her for more information about her employer—the town's newest gossip topic: Sam Calloway.

"Well, uh, Sam can be a little strange," Sunny remarked truthfully.

Strange? Sunny wasn't sure what else to call him. *Aloof? Cranky?* Sam barely made eye contact with her during their brief hellos and good-byes and throughout the entire week communicated more through brusque, handwritten notes than in actual person. But for some reason, she hadn't been able to shake that glimpse of tenderness she'd seen in Sam's eyes when she'd first brought him lunch last week. Surely that had to mean there was a human bone in his body, right?

Kim opened a bag of hamster food, then looked over with a grin. "Yeah, I'd say Sam's strange. He hired you as his children's nanny, didn't he?"

She shot her friend a withering look. "Tee-hee. I'm serious, Kim. Sam doesn't say very much to me at all. Don't you think that's odd?"

"No. Most men aren't talkative."

"But he stares out his window a lot, almost as if he's mad at the world. It can be pretty intense." Sunny shuddered, just thinking about those deep, long looks of his. Sam was obviously a passionate man, and it unnerved her.

But it intrigued her a little bit too.

No, no, don't even let your mind go there, she scolded herself. Sam definitely wasn't giving those intense, long, passionate looks to her. He was probably just staring out the window, thinking about . . . work. Yeah, work. A subject that seemed to be his favorite hobby, pastime, and major food group.

"Well, maybe he's not over the death of his wife," Kim said with a shrug. "It's not unusual for people to become bitter when someone they love dies."

Sunny thought about that. It had never occurred to her that maybe Sam had been thinking of his wife. A funny kind of ache spread throughout her heart, but she brushed off the feeling as sympathy. She knew what it felt like to miss someone that much, and it saddened her to think that a young and handsome man like Sam would have such a hard time moving on with his life. He needed to be strong for his children. She sensed some of their behavioral issues that Sam had mentioned could be caused by their need for more attention and nurturing from him.

"Or maybe he's just one of those deep thinker types," Kim said, interrupting Sunny's thoughts.

"Maybe. More like a *dismal* deep thinker type, though."

"Dismal? Oh, lovely," Kim said with a snort. "Sounds like you're working for a regular Mr. Rochester."

Sunny blinked. "Oh, no, he's not *Jane Eyre* bad," she quickly assured her friend. "In fact, sometimes Sam can be quite sweet." Well, not with her, but with his children, at least. Sweet, cold, tender, gruff—there were such contradictions in Sam's character, Sunny couldn't help but wonder who the real man was. Or why she felt so compelled to try to figure him out.

Kim waved a finger at her. "Well, to be safe, I'd make sure his wife was really dead and not shoved up in an attic somewhere."

"Who's got a dead wife in his attic?" a man's voice asked in alarm.

They both looked over. Josh "Flea" Kaufman, the veterinarian, stood hovering in the doorway. Sunny laughed out loud when she saw the appalled expression plastered all over his ruddy face.

For as long as Sunny could remember, everyone in town

had called the young vet *Flea*. He assured her he got the nickname because he worked with a lot of stray animals, but Sunny assumed it had to do with how tiny in stature the doctor was. Sunny was average height for a woman, and the top of Flea's balding blond head barely grazed her shoulder.

"No one has a dead wife in their attic," Sunny answered, still smiling. "We were just talking about Sam Calloway."

Flea's expression turned sour. "Oh. The new heartthrob in town."

Heartthrob is right. Sunny had heard the talk but, more important, had seen the man enough times in the flesh to legitimize the gossip. "Is that what people are saying?" she asked, trying to keep her tone nonchalant.

Flea walked over to the hamster cage and scooped up Nibbles into his palm. "Oh, come on. The man is rich, handsome, *and* a single father. He seems to be the answer to every marriage-minded woman's prayers around here." As he ran his hand over the hamster's fur, he slanted a concerned look toward Sunny. "Because of that, you should know you're a marked woman."

Sunny gasped. "Marked?"

Flea nodded grimly, placing the hamster back in the cage after inspecting its fur. "I'd pay extra attention when crossing street corners, if I were you. Kelly Green at the cleaners said she was praying you'd break a leg so she could take over your nanny position."

"Why, that little viper," Kim said with a huff, pretending outrage. "She's already moving in on your man."

"Oh, come on." Sunny nudged her halfheartedly in the side. "You know I'm not interested in Sam that way."

Flea's eyebrows shot up. "You aren't?"

"Um, no. No, of course not," Sunny said, feeling stronger

about her statement the more she confirmed it. "Sam is my employer. I take care of his children. It would be unethical for me to want to date him." She bit her lip. "Wouldn't it?"

"I do believe you're right," Flea said, drawing closer to her side. "It would be unethical to get involved with someone you work with, although I've been thinking that—"

"Wow, would you look at the time!" Kim exclaimed as she grabbed Sunny's shoulders and pivoted her body toward the door. "We still need to feed the cats and take the dogs for a walk." She prodded Sunny forward. "Talk to ya later, Flea."

Sunny glanced over her shoulder to say good-bye to Flea, but right at that moment Kim gave her a huge shove through the doorway. Sunny stumbled, then whirled around on her friend, but Kim lifted a finger to her lips and motioned for Sunny to follow her into the cat room.

Kim closed the door behind them, then yanked a Ziploc bag from her pocket. She hadn't even opened the treat bag, yet most of the cats had already formed a small congregation by her feet.

"No need to thank me," Kim said as she sprinkled some of the food onto the floor.

"Thank you?" Sunny asked incredulously. "For throwing my back out? What's going on with you?"

Kim *tsk-tsk*ed. "Oh, dear, that's what I was afraid of. I didn't think you were aware."

"Aware of what?" Sunny held out her hand, and Kim shook some of the cat treats into it. "Flea is sporting a crush on you."

"Flea?" Sunny shook her head. *Impossible.* She and Flea had worked at the shelter together for years and been friends for even longer. He'd never mentioned a thing to her in all that time.

Kim nodded. "I'm afraid so. Kenny Twardski, Jimmy from the post office, not to mention Alan Munford from junior high, and now poor Flea. Oh, honey, I've never seen a woman attract more frogs than princes in my entire life."

Sunny rolled her eyes but realized Kim had a small point. She didn't have a lot of luck attracting men she was interested in dating. Probably because there *hadn't been* any men around she actually wanted to date. Until now. Until . . . maybe . . . Sam.

She mentally smacked herself in the forehead. *No, no, no.* Hadn't she just told Kim and Flea that Sam was off-limits? So the man happened to be a rich, handsome enigma of a father—it didn't mean he was meant for her. What could she possibly offer a man like that? Besides a huge debt to pay off. The man missed his wife too. It was all too unthinkable. Even for someone who believed in fairy tales.

"You know what your problem is?" Kim said. "You're . . . you're just too damn nice."

"What? Since when is being nice a crime?" Sunny said with a laugh. "Besides, I don't think you're right about Flea's feelings for me. He understands we're just friends. But I suppose, to be safe, I'll have to try not being so nice. I don't want to lead him on."

Kim scoffed. "Yeah, like that's going to happen. Flea doesn't stand a chance."

On a sigh, Sunny turned away. Flea was a good guy but not the one for her. She didn't know who "the one" was, but Mom-mom told her when she met him, she'd know. Her prince would come, they'd fall in love, get married, and have a dozen babies—give or take eleven. Mom-mom had always told her to never settle for less.

One of the cats padded up to Sunny and started clawing

the bottom of her flowered jeans. Sunny bent down and stroked its back. The cat's fur felt like velvet between her fingers, and as she rubbed its head, it began to purr. She smiled when the cat stretched out and closed its eyes. There was something so comforting in the way animals showed love toward humans, which drove her thoughts right back to Sam. Hadn't she read somewhere that animals had a way of relieving tension? Maybe Sam needed a pet. Based on their reaction to Oats, his children would probably love to have one too.

"I wonder if he'd like a cat," she murmured aloud.

Kim froze, looking at her as if she'd just spoken Cantonese. "You wonder if *Flea* would like a cat?"

"Uh, no." Sunny stood and avoided making eye contact with her friend by pretending to dust cat hairs off her palm. "Actually, I was talking about Sam."

"Oh, dear. You've worked for this guy for exactly *two* weeks, and already you're thinking about getting him a cat?" Kim clucked her tongue and shook her head. "Uh-uh. Don't do this."

"Don't get Sam a cat?"

"No. Don't go feeling all sympathetic and mushy for him. This is what I was talking about before. You're too nice, and nice girls like you have a way of attaching yourselves to misfits: stray animals, stray men, whatever."

Sunny dismissed her comment with a flick of her wrist. "Don't be silly. Sam could hardly be called a misfit." A loner maybe—an extremely good-looking loner—but certainly not a misfit.

"Oh, Sam's a misfit all right," Kim went on. "The worst kind: a misfit with *baggage*."

Sunny rolled her eyes, but she supposed it could be considered pretty heavy baggage for a man to still be carrying around a torch for his dead wife. But Sunny wasn't looking to compete, just help. Sam was obviously hurting. "Well, misfit or not, I want to do something nice for my employer. After all, he's given me a great job. That's *not* getting attached."

"Well, what else am I supposed to think? You've got that look."

"What look?"

"That look you got exactly five seconds before you became the proud owner of a sixty-five-pound golden retriever with bad breath."

Sunny threw up her chin and sniffed daintily. "I'm glad Oats wasn't around to hear you say that."

Kim chuckled. "I'm just saying this because I know you. You can't resist trying to heal any wounded thing you see. Sam doesn't sound like the type who would appreciate your noble efforts. It's a very nice thought, but my advice to you is to let Sam and his deep, dismal thinking be. I don't want to see you get hurt."

Sunny frowned. *Hurt?* How could she possibly get hurt for trying to be kind to Sam? The thought was ridiculous.

Even though she was annoyed with Kim's quasi-psychoanalysis, she offered her friend a conciliatory smile and hoped to end the conversation. "Look, all I want to do is cheer Sam up a little—if I can. Don't worry. I *won't* get hurt."

"Well . . . okay, because I'd bet all I have that your grandma would come back and haunt me until the day I die if you did."

Sam felt as if he were being haunted.

He sat back at his desk and rubbed his temples. The clock

showed ten after five. The sun was just starting to rise. Sam had gotten maybe four hours of restless sleep before he finally decided to end the misery and get up to do some work in his office.

It was those damn dreams. They'd prevented him from sleeping again. He'd be less concerned if those dreams had to do with his ex-wife, or even an old girlfriend, but no. Instead, his lack of sleep had to do with the blond Mary Poppins who'd been showing up at his door for the past two weeks.

It was unlike him to be so preoccupied with a woman. What was worse was that he'd avoided Sunny all week just so he wouldn't be tempted to think about her, but to no avail. There was something intriguing about her that went beyond the obvious patience she'd shown toward his children or even the kindness she'd shown toward him by bringing him lunch. Her actions had him thinking that maybe she was different—or maybe he'd just been celibate for too long, and it was affecting his brain. *Yeah, that must be it.* Funny, how he'd never had any of those familiar stirrings toward any other nanny he'd hired. But, then again, he'd never hired a nanny who looked like Sunny before.

That compact little body and those wide, perky smiles had his libido at full-blown attention whenever he so much as glanced at her. He'd convinced himself it was curiosity over what his children were up to that had him checking on them throughout the day. He knew better, though. Not that Sunny expressed any interest in him. She was the perfect little employee. The perfect nanny. Which was fine. Wonderful, even. No romantic involvement between co-workers, friends of friends, or your children's nanny was rule number one on his mental "How to avoid sticky complications in life" list. A rule that he should have followed more closely when his mother introduced him to his ex-wife, Kate.

Yeah, he'd learned that one the hard way.

Sam worked clear through Sunny's arrival and well into the afternoon before the doorbell rang and finally stopped him. Sunny and the kids were outside playing, so Sam answered the door, more than a little surprised to see his business partner, Mark Carlstrom.

"Hey, man," Sam said, extending his hand in greeting. "What are you doing down here?"

Mark stepped into his house, took a glance around, and whistled. "I wanted to see how life in the country's been treating you." Then he held out a manila envelope. "And to deliver these to you."

Sam took the paperwork and frowned. "You didn't have to drive two hours to deliver these to me. Not that I don't appreciate the super service, but there is such a thing as FedEx, and I do have a fax machine."

"Yeah, I know, but it was so unlike you to just pick up and leave the company like you did. I wanted to make sure everything was okay. I've had to fend off a lot of questions from our stockholders," Sam's friend said as his gaze traveled around the house again.

Sam felt compelled to look around himself to gauge what his friend was seeing. He took in the hardwood floors Sunny had cleaned that morning, the children's toys scattered in one half of the family room, and Oats' torn bed by the patio door. Overall, his house looked clean yet lived in. Homey. Especially since Sunny had started working there. Quite different from the immaculate condo Sam owned in New York City.

Sam tossed the envelope down on the kitchen island. "Oh, I get it. Now you can report that you saw me with your own eyes, and that I'm alive and well."

Mark walked around, still surveying the house. "Well, I can say you're *alive* at least," he said with a sly grin. "Not so sure about the *well* part yet." He stopped and pointed to the worn dog bed. "You get a dog?"

"Uh, not exactly. It's the nanny's dog." Sam suddenly felt fidgety. What was with all the questions? Sam had known Mark since high school, but he'd never known him to be this fascinated with Sam's personal life before.

Mark looked at him funny, then inhaled deeply through his nose. He arched an eyebrow at Sam, obviously catching the aroma of brownies Sunny had cooling on the kitchen counter. "I see you found a nanny who can bake too. Gee, Sammy, got any freshly squeezed lemonade to go along with this whole Norman Rockwell picture?"

"Actually, hotshot, I do. The woman I hired is pretty handy in the kitchen, and fortunately the kids seem to like her as well."

Sunny marched through the patio doors just then, her long ponytail bouncing along her back and her dog faithfully trailing her every step. "We're out of bubbles," she explained to the two of them before disappearing under the kitchen sink cabinet. "Luckily I brought some glycerin with me for just such an emergency." With a chuckle, she pulled out a large brown bottle. "The kids and I are going to try to make our own from scratch."

Mark flashed a grin and eagerly walked over to her, looking as if she had just announced a plan to solve the nation's oil crisis. Sam was quicker, though—almost tripping over Oats—and stepped in between them.

"Sunny, this is Mark Carlstrom." Sam broke his gaze from her pretty, heat-flushed face and cleared his throat. "Mark, uh, works for me," he explained.

Mark scoffed. "Works for you? You're shortchanging me, man. I just so happen to be your all-around technical guru and eligible-bachelor business partner." He reached around Sam and held out his hand to Sunny. "A real pleasure."

Sunny let out a sweet, tinkling laugh that for some reason grated on Sam's nerves like nails running down a chalkboard when Mark kissed her hand. "Nice to meet you," she said, sounding as though she genuinely meant it and hadn't just said it as a formality.

"And who's this?" Mark asked, when her dog came sniffing at his ankles.

"That's my dog, Oats," she said, giving her a loving pat on the head. "I guess Sam told you I'm the new nanny."

"The nanny?" Mark's eyebrows shot up, and his surprised gaze slid to Sam. "No, as a matter of fact I didn't know that. Sammy boy here never mentioned he hired such a . . . *fun*-looking nanny."

Sam tried to say something but choked on his saliva.

Sunny beamed, obviously not picking up on Mark's hidden meaning of how attractive he thought she was. "That's me. F-U-N." She glanced shyly at Sam. "Well, at least the kids think so. I guess I'd better go see what they're up to." She whirled around with a wave and called out, "Nice meeting you," as she walked away, her dog trotting behind her.

As soon as Sunny slid the patio door closed, Mark folded his arms and shot Sam an accusing look. "Well, well, so *that's* the new nanny."

Sam bristled. "Yeah, so what? What's your point?" He

didn't like what Mark was inferring—like he had done something wrong by hiring a fun, beautiful, young—

Oh, crap. It *did* look bad.

"I hired her for the kids," Sam insisted. "Actually, I didn't even want to hire her in the first place. But the kids got her fired from her old— Look, she's doing a good job."

Mark chuckled. "Sorry, Sam, but I call 'em like I see 'em. When you hire a nanny for the kids, you hire Mrs. Doubtfire. When you hire someone who looks like Sunny . . . well, I'm afraid you hired her for yourself. Not that I blame you," he said with a shrug. "I would have hired her in a New York minute myself. I'm sure it gets lonely out here in the country, and Sunny looks like someone who'd be *very* good company."

"Get your mind out of the gutter." Sam rolled his eyes, but on the inside Mark's semi-lewd comment got to him. He didn't like Sunny being talked about so objectively.

"You've been divorced for over three years, Sammy, and I haven't seen you with a woman since. I was starting to worry about you. I thought maybe you had given up on the opposite sex completely."

"I didn't hire Sunny because of the way she looks. I hired her because she's good with the kids. That's all I want right now."

Mark seemed nonplussed at Sam's prickly denial. "Whatever you say. I should get going now anyhow. I promised my sister I'd bring her back some of that famous boardwalk fudge." He sauntered over to the patio doors and peered out into the backyard. "But, uh, seeing how you're not interested in pursuing the convenience of having a beautiful woman in your home, I guess you won't mind me leaving through the back so I can say good-bye to Sunny personally." He cracked his knuckles and grinned. "Maybe I can work the ol' charm on her."

"You're not working anything on her." Sam saw red but kept his voice low.

"Why? Is she seeing someone?"

Sam didn't know. He shouldn't care. But suddenly the idea of Sunny seeing Mark or anyone else for that matter made him crazy. "Just back off."

Mark paused, looking as though his own temper was riled. But after another moment, he drew himself up straight and met Sam's eyes calmly. "All right," he finally said. "But I think you'd better take a long look at yourself, my friend, and analyze why—for someone *not* interested in Sunny— you're about ready to crack me one in the mouth."

Sam's jaw grew slack, and he looked down at his hands— which had involuntarily clenched into fists. He dropped his arms to his side. Dammit. He felt foolish and angry at himself for displaying such an uncharacteristic flare of posses- siveness toward a woman he barely knew—a woman he'd convinced himself he didn't *want* to know.

Mark clapped his friend sympathetically on the back. Without saying a word, he walked over to the front door and opened it. "Enjoy your time away from the city, Sammy," he called over his shoulder. Then he added, "I know *I* would."

Chapter Five

"These bubbles don't work," Emma protested.

"Yes, they do." Cole grabbed the bubble bottle from Emma's chubby hand. "You're not blowing hard enough." He proceeded to show his sister, blowing his little heart out until one tiny bubble finally emerged from the wand.

Sunny covered her smile with her hand. "Um, here. Allow me." Cole handed her the bubbles. "If you're having problems, you can always cheat like I do."

Emma giggled. "You're so silly. You can't cheat at blowing bubbles."

"Sure you can," Sunny said with a wink. "You don't blow." She showed them what she meant by dipping the wand in the bubbles, then slowly waving it in the air. A long stream of bubbles blew out before them. The children laughed, and when the bubbles disappeared, they begged Sunny to make some more, which she readily did. Emma and Cole went chasing after them, trying to pop as many of them in their hands as they could.

Sunny sat down on the patio step, enjoying the warm

breeze coming off the bay. It was nice to get a break like this. She and the children had been playing knight and princesses for the past hour. Emma insisted Sunny wear the Princess Miranda shoes Sunny had given to her that first day she'd met them at the boardwalk. Emma played her little princess daughter, and Cole was the knight who had to defend them from all the nefarious things that threatened their kingdom—which comprised of a couple of Webkinz stuffed animals, a Spider-Man action figure, and a rather large dead tree branch.

"That was way cool," Cole said, running back up to her when the bubbles had disappeared. "Do it again."

Sunny beamed, dipping the bubble wand into the bubbles and waving it in the air again. The wind lifted the bubbles, and Cole ran off again, trying to catch them.

"Your arm is going to get tired."

Sam's voice directly behind her made her jump. His husky tone made her heart leap too. Because of that wayward response, Sunny didn't dare turn around. "Oh, I don't mind. I can go at it all day." She winced at her choice of phrasing.

He made a simple comment to you, you dope. Try not to sound like Julia Roberts in Pretty Woman.

Sam slid the screen door open and stepped outside. "Well, that's good. It's nice to know you have such . . . stamina," he said, taking a seat next to her on the patio.

"Um, right. I meant my arm. My arm has lots of stamina." She waved her wrist and made a couple of throwing motions to prove her point. "That's what I meant when, uh, I said . . ."

Sam's lips quirked into a grin so appealing, she lost her train of thought. She looked away, knowing if she didn't, she'd only embarrass herself further.

She couldn't help feeling flustered. Usually Sam was so

curt in his responses to her. This was the first time he had ever gone out of his way to talk to her—or in this case *sit* with her.

She wondered if there was a problem he needed to talk to her about. Had she done something wrong? With a little unease, she stole a glance at him, and a little sigh escaped her lips. Sam was so handsome, and the smile that illuminated his face as he watched his children chase bubbles in the yard melted her heart toward him even further. He loved his children; it showed whenever they were near him. Too bad his work didn't allow him to spend more time with them.

She quickly cleared her throat. "Um, was there something you wanted to speak to me about?"

Sam nodded. "I know I haven't said this to you before now," he told her, shifting his attention from his children to his folded hands, "but I wanted you to know that I think you're doing a great job for me—well, for the kids. I don't think I—I mean, *they've* eaten so well in months."

Sunny almost forgot to breathe. Sam thought she was doing her job well—not only that, but she found it rather endearing that a man like him would seem almost shy in telling her. "Well, it's my pleasure. It's kind of nice to use Mommom's recipes again. Since she died, I don't bother cooking for myself. Most nights it's usually just soup from a can." Sunny didn't bother to mention that it was cheaper to eat that way, too. Which brought her to the next topic.

"Uh, Sam, I meant to ask you something as well. It's been two weeks, and I was wondering . . ."

A wry smile touched his lips. "I suppose you'd like to get paid, huh?"

"Yes." At the risk of sounding as desperate as she was, she didn't hesitate to answer.

He chuckled and pulled out a folded check from his shirt pocket. "I think from what we discussed, you'll find the amount fair. But we can always negotiate if you like."

Sunny took the check from his hand. Their fingertips gently brushed together, and her stomach muscles tightened. *So much for that zing of attraction being a fluke,* she thought worriedly. To make sure she didn't accidentally touch him again, she scooted a few inches away from him. Then she unfolded the check, and her eyes widened when she saw the dollar amount. Speechless, she gazed back up at Sam.

Sam's brows furrowed. "Well, like I said, the amount can be negotiated."

Sunny shook her head, still unable to find her voice. Was he kidding? It was as if she'd hit the lottery! And if she had her voice, she would have shouted for joy. She'd never handled a check this size before and could not even fathom getting more of them just like it.

Impulsively, she leaned over and kissed him on the cheek. Her breath caught when she realized what she had done. The contact was brief, but her lips were still humming from the rough feel of his five o'clock shadow. She raised a hand to her mouth, an apology on the tip of her tongue, but Sam spoke first.

"Good. Fine," he said in a gruff voice, then turned his attention back to the children. He cleared his throat. "I'm glad you're happy with your salary, because I'd like to keep you on for the entire summer."

Sunny clasped her hands together and beamed. "Do you mean it? Oh, I was hoping you'd say that. I already planned so many fun things we could do together. I even borrowed some books from the library on kids' crafts. Maybe I could take them to the animal shelter. Oh, and there's—"

"Easy does it." Sam laughed, and the deep, rich sound of it poured over her like hot fudge. "It's too late for a raise, you know. You already said you're happy with your salary."

Her face warmed. "Sorry. I'm just so excited to have a job. Especially a job I enjoy. I really love taking care of Emma and Cole." *And you.*

Sunny blinked. *And you?* Oh, no! Where had *that* thought come from?

"Well, I can tell you love your job by how happy Emma and Cole are," Sam said, gesturing to the children. Then he glanced back over to her and frowned. "Hey, are you feeling all right?" He shifted closer and was about to lay his hand on her cheek, but she bolted to her feet before he could touch her.

"I'm fine!" She practically screamed her answer, indicating to Sam, the children, and half his neighbors that she was far from being fine. No, she was *not* fine. In fact, she was light-headed, and her heart felt like it was going to shoot out of her chest at the mere thought of Sam so much as laying a finger on her cheek.

"It's hot out," she blurted. She waved her hands in front of her face. "I think I just need a cool drink." A *stiff* drink, more likely. Maybe a double.

"Here," he said, lifting his glass of iced tea that he had brought outside with him. "Drink some."

Sunny almost rolled her eyes. She didn't need his iced tea. She needed him to go back to his cave of an office and ignore her like he usually did. But she took the tea and tentatively brought the glass up to her lips. When the cool liquid slid down her throat, she was surprised to find that it did make her feel a little calmer. She sat back down, silently admonishing herself for being so unprofessional and not controlling her visceral response to him. "Thanks," she said weakly.

"I should really be thanking you. You know, I already see a difference in Emma and Cole's behavior."

Sunny had noticed a difference in their behavior too. Emma wasn't as whiny. Cole controlled his temper better. But she could hardly allow Sam to let her take all the credit. "You know, Sam, I think the children are happier because you're around them more. Sometimes Oats acts very badly when I ignore her or leave her alone for too long."

He heaved a frustrated sigh. "My job is time consuming, but because of it I can give them a lot more than most children their age. I want—no, I *need*—to provide that for them."

How about what the children want and need? she wanted to ask, but she wisely kept her mouth shut. She already knew Sam was not a man who liked to be lectured, and she wanted to keep her job. So instead she asked, "Um, what exactly is your job?"

Sam's brows shot up. "You honestly don't know? I would've thought half the town saw that article about me in the *Times*."

Sunny shrugged. Not that they lived in a proverbial box, but most people—including herself—in Ocean Bluff read the *Bluff Gazette*, the town newspaper.

"You're serious." He scratched his head, then let out a laugh. "When we first met I thought . . . Well, Mark and I created and run Mambo.com." When she just stared at him, he added, "The largest and best search engine in the world."

"Oh, I see. Like Google?"

Sam's eyes narrowed, and he held up a finger. "Uh-uh. Don't ever say the *G* word around me."

"Sorry." Sunny ducked her chin to hide her smile. "Won't happen again."

"So, do you use it?" Sam asked.

"Well, no. Actually, I don't own a computer. But I've been taking a lot of odd jobs right now, so maybe I'll be able to buy one soon." *Like in about three to five years. Maybe.*

Sam frowned. "Why do you need another job? I thought we agreed that what I'm paying you—"

"No, no, it's not about the money," she lied. *Sheesh.* Half the town might know about her current financial mess, but that didn't mean Sam had to know too. She did have *some* pride left. "Um, I like working. It keeps me busy and . . . out of trouble."

Amusement danced in his eyes. "You don't look like much of a troublemaker to me."

She blushed. "Well, if my grandmom was alive, she'd tell you differently, I'm sure."

Emma and Cole came running over just then, looking excited to see their father out of his office and enjoying the remaining afternoon daylight. "Daddy, did you see all the bubbles Sunny made?" Emma asked, her cheeks rosy from running.

"They landed on the grass, and we stomped on them like Godzilla," Cole added.

Sam chuckled and nodded. "I did. It looked like—" Sam's cell phone interrupted their conversation. His eyebrows pulled together as he whipped the phone out of his pocket and checked to see who was calling.

"I have to take this," he said to them. "It'll just be a minute." He stood, placing the phone up to his ear, and stepped back into the house.

Emma and Cole's faces fell as they watched their father

disappear into the house. "It's never just a minute," Emma said sadly as she walked over to the swings.

Then Cole turned away and kicked his ball so hard, it landed in the bay. Sunny was about to reprimand him, but the disappointment in his eyes stopped her cold. They obviously wanted to spend more time with their dad. Sunny's heart went out to them. Maybe it wasn't her place, but she would have to have a talk with Sam about his workaholic ways. And soon.

Warm wind blew through Sunny's hair as she pedaled her bicycle toward Sam's house a few days later. She let the handlebars go and spread out her arms, enjoying the sun's blanket of warmth on her skin. It was a beautiful morning, but the day was only going to get hotter, so she made sure she was armed and ready for her afternoon swimming activity with the kids.

She'd promised Emma and Cole days ago that when the bay water was warm enough, she'd take them out. So she called Kim and packed her floaties, grateful for the fact that both of Sam's children could swim without assistance. Otherwise, this plan would never work. Sunny didn't have the heart to disappoint the children just because she'd never learned how to swim.

Once Sunny reached Sam's house, she grabbed her bag of swimming items and walked her bike around back. The back patio door was open, so she let herself in.

"Ding-dong," she said, grinning at her own makeshift doorbell greeting.

"Sunny!" Emma exclaimed, shoving her bowl of cereal away and jumping out of her chair. "Are we swimming today? Please! Please! You *pwomised*."

"Yeah," Cole said. "You promised. So are we, Sunny?"

Sunny laughed at their elephant memories. "Yes, yes." She lifted her swim bag before them. "Today is officially the day."

"Yay!" they cried, dancing around the kitchen.

Sam walked in the room then, dark eyebrows pulled together in a deep V—like the Grinch himself ready to steal the fun out of summer from every Who in Whoville. "Today is officially the day for *what*?" he asked, frowning.

Sunny's shoulders tensed at his sharp questioning. *Good morning to you too*, she thought dryly. She was so convinced that she and Sam had made such progress in getting to know each other last week. He'd shared some of his personal life with her, and she had with him.

Now, for whatever reason, they were back to square one. Obviously that little talk she wanted to have with Sam about spending time with the kids was going to have to wait now.

Why couldn't he greet her with a smile one time this week? One time! Was that so much to ask for? He was so frustrating, she could just kick him. But then she heard Mom-mom's voice echo in her head. *Don't you mind people like that. People act like that 'cause they're sad inside. Try to make them forget their troubles, Princess.*

Make him forget his troubles? What was she supposed to do, pull a coin out of his ear? When Mom-mom had given her that advice, she obviously had never come across a man as moody as Sam Calloway.

Sunny fiddled with her bag for a moment, then remembered that Sam had asked her a question. "Oh. Um, today is the official day I promised to take the kids swimming in the bay."

She didn't think it was humanly possible, but Sam's brow furrowed deeper. "Swimming?"

"Yeah. I hope you don't mind, but I invited Kim and her son to swim with us." She summoned up a small nervous smile and lifted her suit out of her swim bag. "I brought my bathing suit." And floaties. And nose plugs. And swimmer's ear medication. She sighed. She was beginning to think this wasn't such a hot idea now.

Sam nodded, looking everywhere but at her and the bathing suit she held up. "That's fine. Well . . . have fun." He walked over to Emma and Cole and planted kisses on top of each of their heads. "You listen to Sunny," he said to them. "Stay close to the dock."

Emma grabbed his arm to keep him from walking to his office. "Oh, I listen real good, Daddy. Yesterday, Sunny only had to tell me three times not to stand on the table."

"Very good, but let's try to make it only two times today, okay?" Sam said.

Emma and Cole nodded and ran off, and Sam shook his head with a chuckle. Sunny couldn't help but notice that whenever Sam smiled, the dark circles under his eyes diminished, and the blue in his gray eyes became more pronounced. All the harsh lines in his face disappeared and left just . . . Sam—a man who for some reason wanted to hide that gentle side of himself.

"You know what?" Sunny blurted.

"What?" Sam cocked an eyebrow and folded his arms, trying to go back to his I'm-a-big-bully stare.

Sunny folded her arms right back at him. *Uh-uh.* This time, she wasn't fooled. She knew there was softness underneath that gruff demeanor.

"You should"—she waved her finger toward his mouth area—"do that more."

"Do what?" Sam swiped at his lips and chin, as if he thought he had crumbs on his face.

"No, no." She laughed. "*Smile.* I think you should smile more. You have a really nice one."

The corners of Sam's mouth kicked up, and that so-called *nice* smile she was just talking about suddenly turned sexy and bone-melting before she could blink. "Thank you," he said huskily.

She gulped. "Um, you're welcome. I just think you should practice smiling more . . . you know, seeing how I seem to make you frown so much and all." *Ooops. Stop babbling, you dummy.* She cleared her throat. "Um, because you know what they say. You don't use it, you lose it."

Sam cocked his head and looked at her thoughtfully. "I'll try to keep that in mind."

"Thanks for coming over with Tommy," Sunny said after she blew a lungful of air into her inner tube. She stole a glance at her floatie progress. Would this thing even hold her? She quickly felt the tube's sturdiness. Oh, goodness. She hoped so.

Kim turned around to shield herself from Tommy's splash as he dove off the dock. Emma and Cole swam up and splashed him as soon as he resurfaced.

"My pleasure," Kim said, drying off her sunglasses with the corner of her bathing suit cover-up. "It's not often I'm asked to take time out of my day to come to a beautiful bayside house and play lifeguard."

"Well, even if nobody drowns, you're still a lifesaver in my book." She leaned in and whispered, "I didn't want to disappoint the kids just because of my, uh, problem."

"Not being able to swim is hardly a problem."

"Shh!" Sunny admonished. "I don't want them to know I can't swim. It's embarrassing."

Kim rolled her eyes. "Whatever. But I find it quite comical that you promised the kids you'd go swimming with them anyway. I told you that you were too nice."

Sunny stuck out her tongue. "Okay. Maybe I am. But look how much fun they're having."

Kim looked out at Emma and Cole swimming around the dock, playing Marco Polo, and smiled. Even Tommy, who was fifteen, was enjoying playing with the kids. "Yeah. What a great day to be outside."

Sunny suddenly thought of Sam cooped up in the house, working diligently and missing out on this beautiful summer day with his family. She couldn't resist gazing up toward his office window.

He was there, watching the whole display with a small smile lingering on his lips. He looked to be talking on his phone as he did so. Sunny lifted her hand to get his attention, but he disappeared again as soon as she was about to wave.

Oh, well. No big surprise that Mr. Big City Internet Giant was too busy to watch. At least he wouldn't be there to witness her make a spectacle of herself as she tried to get into the water with a pink and blue floatie glued to her waist. *If* she tried to get into the water. She could feel her chest tightening up just kicking the idea around in her head. She wished Mom-mom had pushed her more into swim lessons. When Sunny was a child, she was petrified of the water, and Mom-mom, being just as much a softy as she was tough, never had the heart to push Sunny into something that frightened her so much.

Kim sat down on the dock, letting her feet dangle in the

water. "Come on. Put your feet in, at least. The water feels great."

Sunny bit her lip. The water did look inviting, and she was so hot. But what if she slipped?

"Oh, come on, the water's not going to bite," Kim said, splashing her.

"Okay, okay." Sunny knelt down and tentatively put one foot in at a time. "Oooh, this does feel good. Hey, I'm glad I thought of it," she said with a teasing grin.

Kim laughed and splashed her again.

"Watch me, Sunny," Emma called as she floated on her back.

"No, look at me, Sunny!" Cole shouted as he dove underwater.

Sunny grabbed Kim's arm. "Oh gosh, should I allow him to do that? He could drown."

"Relax," Kim said, patting her hand. "Cole's fine. He's a good swimmer."

Sunny's shoulders relaxed, and she was able to take a deep breath. Cole and Emma were actually *both* really good swimmers. And Kim and her son, Tommy, were there in case there was a problem. She didn't know why she was so worried, but she didn't know what she'd do if something happened to those kids. They were beginning to mean something more to her than just a job.

And their father is beginning to mean something to you too, a little voice in her head said.

Sunny blinked.

Well, she supposed it was only natural to think fondly of her employer too. But that was all. She turned her head and stole another peek at Sam's window. He hadn't come back to watch. She didn't know what to think about why she hoped he would.

"I'm hungry," Kim said, jarring Sunny from her thoughts.

"You're . . . huh?"

"Not *huh*. Huh-n-gree. You got any snacks in that big Sub-Zero fridge of Sam's?"

"Well, I have some fruit salad left over. Oh, and there's some of my white-bean dip."

Kim's face brightened. "Oooh, I love that stuff." She pulled her legs out of the water and stood. "I'm going to the bathroom, and then I'll bring us out some munchies. I bet the kids could use a snack too."

Sunny's stomach rumbled on cue. "Make sure you bring enough for all of us."

"I need to use the potty," Emma called, swimming up to them.

Sunny looked at Kim. "Would you mind taking her, since you're going in?"

"Not at all." When Emma climbed onto the dock, Kim wrapped her in a fluffy Snow White towel, then they walked toward the house together.

Sunny leaned back against her arms, moving her legs back and forth in the water, enjoying the coolness of it against her heated body. Her gaze traveled down. *Uh-oh.* Her thighs looked to be getting red. She was about to reach for her sunscreen when Tommy and Cole came swimming up to her with big grins on their faces.

"Aunt Sunny, why are you still dry?" Tommy asked mischievously, casting a sidelong glance toward Cole.

Sunny held up her hands to shield herself, afraid they would splash her at any second. "Don't even think about it, sport. I'm not used to the water yet."

"Well, maybe we can help you get used to it." Tommy gave a short nod to Cole, and then, before she realized what was happening, both of them grabbed her legs and pulled.

Sunny fell in with a water-garbled scream. As soon as she went under, her arms froze, and immediately her body felt as if two boulders had been attached to her legs. She gasped for breath and choked. Her lungs began to burn.

That was the last thing she remembered.

Chapter Six

Sam's hands trembled as he wrapped Sunny with the closest towel he could find. He carefully laid her down on the dock and knelt beside her, turning her head to the side so that any water could drain from her mouth. Adrenaline hummed through his body. Positioning Sunny's head forward again, he breathed into her mouth four times, then pulled back to check her pulse.

Sam could barely process what was happening around him—Sunny unconscious, Cole and Tommy with frightened faces, Emma crying in the background while Kim tried her best to comfort her. Sam struggled to catch his breath. He would tend to his children, but first he had to collect himself and make sure Sunny hadn't stopped breathing.

"Am I dead?" Sunny suddenly croaked.

He hung his head and let out a nervous chuckle. *Thank God she was all right. Just . . . thank God.*

He quickly composed himself, then pinned her with a hard stare. "No, you're not dead, but you're going to *wish* you were when I get through with you."

Sunny tried to smile at that but suddenly looked to be in pain. She turned her head and coughed up some water. Her body began to shake, and she curled over on her side. Sam quickly grabbed another towel for her, holding it on her shoulders with widespread hands.

He looked at Kim. "Just what the heck happened?" he growled.

Tommy stepped forward, nervously chewing the end of the towel he had wrapped around himself. "We didn't know she'd freak out like that, Mr. Calloway. Cole and I were just playing around. We didn't mean to hurt her."

Sunny turned over onto her back again with a groan. Sam rubbed a hand over his face and took a deep breath, trying to get a handle on the tense sickness swirling in his stomach. Before he spoke, he had to remind himself that Sunny *wasn't* hurt. She was okay. "All right," he said with a sigh. "She's fine, boys. I'm going to take her inside so she can lie down a bit. But I think she's had enough swimming for today."

Emma broke away from Kim's arms and walked over to him, tears still clinging to her big blue eyes. "I don't want to swim anymore today, Daddy. I don't want to be in my bathing suit anymore either."

Sam pulled his daughter into his arms. "Okay. Whatever you want, baby," he soothed. He kissed her forehead and hugged her tightly, hoping to ease the distress of seeing her nanny pulled from the water unconscious. After their mother died, he'd worked hard to protect them from ever going through this kind of pain again. He thought he had done a good job of it too. Obviously not good enough.

"I'll help Emma change," Kim offered. "It's the least I can do. I feel terrible about Tommy scaring her like that."

Sam shook his head. "Don't worry about it. It was an accident. But, yeah, if you could help Emma change for me. I'll take Sunny inside." Kim nodded and led Emma by the hand to the house. Sam then looked at Cole, hoping to offer some comfort to him as well.

"I'm sorry, Daddy," he said, his little mouth trembling. "We thought Sunny could swim."

Sam smiled sympathetically. Of course they thought Sunny could swim. Anyone in their right mind would have assumed the same thing. And now Sam wanted to know why she hadn't mentioned that little tidbit of information before. The only person who'd seemed to know was Kim. No wonder Sunny had invited her along for the afternoon.

"It's okay," he calmly told his son. Sam reached out and laid a hand on his son's shoulder and squeezed it to reassure him. "You didn't know. Everything will be all right. Why don't you and Tommy go change now too?"

Cole nodded, and the boys walked toward the house.

Sam gazed down at Sunny, resting there with her eyes closed and her hands clasped together to her chest. She looked as if she were an angel praying. He was struck by how serene she seemed after her near-death experience. The poor girl must have had the fright of her life.

Who was he kidding? *He* had just had the fright of his life.

Sam had to touch her then. He leaned in and gently ran his knuckles over her pale, damp cheeks and neck, grateful for the faint pulse he felt underneath his fingers. He'd never been so scared as when he saw Sunny go under the water and then not come up. He feared she'd gotten a swimmer's cramp or maybe had her foot tangled on something at the bottom of the bay. But then he heard Kim yell from the kitchen,

"She can't swim!" and he just about had a heart attack. Without thinking, he'd rushed out of the house and jumped into the water.

Just considering what might have happened made Sam swear out loud. Sunny's eyes were still closed, but he noticed her wince in response. *Good*, he thought. Her ears were working perfectly. She should know how angry he was with her. What was she trying to prove by promising to take his children swimming when she didn't know how to swim? That she was a pushover and couldn't say no? Or that she was the kind of woman who would do almost anything to keep her job? He didn't know what to think about her now, or even how to feel about her.

Except that he *did* feel something for her.

He couldn't deny he was attracted to Sunny, and from the conversation they'd had the other week, it seemed as if Sunny was attracted to him too. But damn if he knew what he wanted to do about it. His friend Mark had certainly made it clear what *he* would do if he was in the same circumstance, but Mark hadn't had the same experiences with women Sam had, hadn't had the reason to doubt women like Sam had. Sam just wasn't sure he was ready to open up again this soon.

Sam tossed aside the towel, then gathered Sunny up in his arms and stood. Surprised by her weight, he swayed back a step. For such a little thing, Sunny certainly wasn't light, and he almost smiled as he shifted her in his arms to get a better hold of her.

Once he had a secure grip, he began carrying her toward the patio. He was only able to take a few steps before Sunny placed her hand on his chest to stop him. But when she opened her mouth, she turned her face and let out a string of rough coughs.

"I'm fine, Sam," she said hoarsely. "You can put me down now."

Put her down?

Sam rolled his eyes. *Yeah, right.* He ignored her and kept walking.

The woman almost drowns at his home, and she expects him to let her parade around his backyard as if she'd just been through a slight inconvenience. Not a chance. His hands tightened instinctively. There was no way he was going to let go of her now. She needed medical attention. If anything, he needed to make sure she didn't accidentally walk into the bay again. He also needed to hold on to her a little longer for his own piece of mind—to make sure she was okay, that she was still safe. Alive.

"You're all wet," Sunny said with confusion, lightly mopping up the beads of water running down the sides of his face with her fingers.

"Yeah, well, that's what happens when you're forced to take an impromptu dip in the bay," he snapped.

Sam kept his gaze focused straight ahead, but he could feel Sunny's shocked stare. He wasn't going to apologize for snapping at her, though. He knew his tone was harsh, but it was the only way he could deal with the rainbow array of emotions going through his system. She had put his children at risk. She had put *herself* at risk. What if something more serious had happened?

He reached the patio door and slid it open with his foot. As soon as he stepped into the kitchen, he slowly placed Sunny on her feet, allowing his hands to waver a few inches away from her arms in case she wobbled and needed him to catch her.

"I think we should get you to a hospital," he told her.

Her eyes snapped up to his, and her face turned a degree paler. "I cannot go to the hospital."

Her adamant refusal gave him pause. "What are you talking about? You almost drowned. You have to get checked out to make sure you're okay."

"No. I can't afford— Uh, I can't afford to leave Oatsie at the house by herself for so long. You know how backed up hospitals are. Besides, like I told you, I'm fine now."

Sam stared at her through narrowed eyes. Sunny's flimsy excuse didn't sit well with him, but he decided not to press her on it. The woman had been through enough. He'd have to make sure Kim stayed with her through the night, just to be on the safe side.

"All right," he agreed. "No hospital."

Sunny smiled, then her expression turned dazed as she took in his drenched ensemble—from the olive polo shirt plastered against his chest all the way down to his soaked shoes and socks. Self-consciously, he ran a hand through his wet hair.

He read the dawning of what he had done for her— jumping in and pulling her out of the bay—written all over her lovely face. She slowly tipped her chin up toward him. Her gaze locked with his, and that protective barrier he had so carefully placed around his heart cracked.

"Thank you," she whispered in awe.

A sweet vulnerability—something more than just gratefulness—showed in her beautiful blue-green eyes then, and suddenly Sam couldn't breathe. He swallowed hard. All the suspicions and questions about her prickled the back of his mind, yet he took a step forward. She licked her lips, and her gaze dropped to his mouth. He knew it was crazy, what he was about to do. But at that moment, he just didn't care.

"Sunny . . ." he murmured, allowing his hands to travel up her cool, bare arms. That simple touch of her skin felt so good to him. Or maybe it was the anticipation of what was to come, what he realized he wanted so badly. His fingers tightened on her shoulders, and he pulled her into him. Her body tensed, but she didn't push away. She just continued to watch him as he leaned his face in closer to hers. Then slowly and gently, he touched his lips to hers.

Her mouth parted, and their tongues touched for just a few seconds. He heard her half sigh, half moan into his mouth, and as he sank deeper, he couldn't have agreed with her more.

She tasted heavenly—part angel, part sunshine, part desirable woman—and he wanted all of her.

Sunny's arms reached up and wrapped around his neck, and the towel she had draped around her body dropped to her feet. She stood in only her bathing suit now—nothing as risqué as some of the ones he'd seen worn by sunbathers in Central Park, but it was completely backless. Sam took the opportunity to run his hands over her moist, warm skin, but was brought back to reality when he heard Emma running in the hallway upstairs. He realized he was getting himself into territory that could embarrass both him and Sunny and compromise their professional relationship if he continued any further.

He stilled his hands, then gently eased back. "You should go change."

"Hmm?" she murmured dreamily.

When her eyes remained closed, he had to smile. Obviously, she didn't want the kiss to end any more than he did. But, however pleasurable their kiss was, it had to end sometime. He was a realist. It was ridiculous to think he would pursue a relationship with his children's nanny. Her near-drowning may have weakened him and caused him to give in to his attraction, but his brain was fully functioning now. That kiss they'd shared had just been an indulgence.

One he needed to put behind him. Something that good never lasted anyway.

He cleared his throat. "And you need swim lessons," he added roughly.

Her eyes sprang open at that. "What?" She looked so adorable with cheeks flushed pink and her eyes round like buttons that he wanted to forget all about that indulgence crap and kiss her all over again.

Pull yourself together, Calloway. It was just a kiss.

He dropped his arms and took another step back. "Why didn't you tell me you couldn't swim, Sunny? For goodness' sake, my children have been through enough trauma in their little lives. They didn't need to see their nanny almost drown."

Sunny picked up her fallen towel and wrapped it around herself. "I know. I'm sorry," she said quietly. "I would never do anything to hurt your kids. It's just that they really wanted to go swimming and I figured Kim was there to be life-guard and well, I—I didn't mean to almost drown."

"Oh, well, that's just *great*." Sam threw his hands up in the air and spun away. "She didn't mean to almost drown," he murmured to himself. He looked back at her, his anger growing along with the strange desire to pull her into his arms and tell her it was okay.

"I should fire you" came out of his mouth instead.

She gasped. "Oh, please don't." Tears sprang into her eyes. "I'll never take the children swimming—or even *near* the bay again. We'll never even go outside again. Anything you want."

Sam turned away. Heck, he *should* fire her. Get her out of his house, his mind, and his life once and for all. But he wouldn't. He obviously was too much of a glutton for punishment. Besides, the children loved her. Plus, deep down inside, Sam knew Sunny would never do anything intentional to hurt them.

"Fine," he snapped. "But since this house is on the bay and you're watching my children, I want you to take swim lessons."

She flinched, not noticing that her towel had slipped off again. "Oh, uh, I can't take swim lessons," she protested, twisting her hands in front of her. "I—I've tried before. They—they, um, didn't take."

He bent down and picked up her towel off the floor, wrapping it around her shoulders again. "They'll take this time," he assured her. "Because I'm personally going to teach you."

"*You?*" she said, her eyes growing wide. "Oh, no. You're too busy. I couldn't—"

He stilled her protests with a finger across her lips. Damn, but her mouth was soft. It was a mistake to touch her like this, but so was offering her personalized swim lessons. It went along with the whole glutton-for-punishment thing, he supposed.

He removed his hand from her mouth and folded his arms. "I insist. I'll teach you Saturday mornings. Nine o'clock sharp. Besides, my kids will enjoy seeing you here on Saturdays as well."

She bit her lip. "I don't know. . . ."

Sam hadn't gotten where he was in his business by rolling over and playing dead; he tried a different tack. "Sunny, if nothing else, let me *try* to teach you so we don't have a

repeat performance of your impersonation of an anchor."
He pulled up the hem of his soaked pants and held out his
ankle, showing her his ruined shoes. "I only packed one
other pair of suede bucks," he said wryly.

His joke didn't ease any of her obvious anxiety. She looked
away, lowering her gaze to the floor. He thought she'd protest
again, but after a long moment she finally said, "Okay. I
work at the animal shelter on Saturday mornings, though.
I—I guess I could stop by afterward." She shot him a shaky
smile. "Maybe around noon next week?"

He nodded. "It's a date."

"Um, then he said, 'It's a date.'"

The next day Sunny relayed the whole play-by-play scene
she'd had with Sam—minus the kiss, of course—to Kim
while they were working at the animal shelter. Mrs. Brinkman, who worked in the dress shop across the street, happened to come in and hear the story too.

Kim shook her head in wonder. "I don't know what I'm
more shocked to hear—you willing to take swim lessons or
Sam Calloway willing to teach you."

"I have to admit, I'm a little shocked myself." *Shocked?*
That was an understatement. There was no way on earth
she wanted to get back into that water—but the way Sam
had tenderly held and kissed her lingered in her system like
a drug-induced haze and obviously sent her ability to make
logical decisions right out the window.

"Let me tell you, I never saw a man of his size move so
fast," Kim said with a chuckle.

Mrs. Brinkman raised her eyebrows, looking impressed.
"You don't say. Sam Calloway is a rather large man. Bet he
played football in college."

"I don't know about football," Kim told them. "From my perspective, I'd say he was a record-holder on the track team. He flew right past me out the door and dove in—shoes and all—even though Tommy had already grabbed Sunny and was pulling her back to the dock."

Mrs. Brinkman held her palms to her cheeks. "That must have been quite a sight for everybody."

Sunny stifled a laugh, remembering how endearing Sam had looked that day sloshing back to the house with his wet hair dripping and curling around his forehead and neck. Sunny was glad she could find humor in the situation now. It was kind of sexy, the way his wet clothes hugged each and every inch of his body. Sam had a nice, toned body she would have never discovered otherwise. Unfortunately, she let that body sidetrack her too much. She had done a lot of crazy things in her life—including almost drowning—but kissing a man like Sam Calloway had to be number two or three on her all-time list of craziest.

Mrs. Brinkman shot Sunny a sly smile. "If I didn't know better, honey, I'd say that man is sweet on you."

Sunny's heart skipped a beat, but she tried to play it casual. "Oh, I don't know. . . . Do you really think so? But he's this mega-Internet superrich guy, and I'm . . . I'm . . ."

What was she?

A woman who worked two jobs and still could barely afford to feed her dog? She sighed. What was she thinking? She had no right to think Sam had any serious interest in her. She obviously had been playing princess and dreaming of fairy tales for far too long.

"You're a sweet and lovely girl," Mrs. Brinkman said, finishing Sunny's sentence.

She tried a small smile. In Sam's world "sweet and lovely"

were the same as "boring and invisible." "Thanks. But Sam's just a friend."

Kim folded her arms, shooting Sunny her best Mommy Dearest scowl. "Well, that's good to hear, because once summer is gone, Sam and the kids will be gone too. Just remember that."

"Right." Sunny had remembered that even before Kim said it. Even before Sam had reminded her of it the other day. She would be wise to repeat that to herself a few times a day just to be sure she didn't end up way over her head. The kiss they shared was proof enough that she had it bad for him.

The bell above the front door jingled. Already feeling like she'd been kicked in the teeth, Sunny watched her morning get worse when Kelly Green from the cleaners strolled in. "Oh, you poor thing," Kelly said, clasping her hands together in fake concern. "How scary for the children. I heard about your near drowning."

"You did?" Sunny asked, glancing over at Kim.

Kim smiled feebly. "News travels fast, huh?"

"What are you talking about?" Kelly said, planting both fists on her hips. "You told me yourself this morning at the coffee shop."

Sunny threw her hands up in the air. "Thanks a lot, Kim. Now the whole town probably knows what happened to me. How embarrassing."

Kelly's eyes took on a sudden gleam. "What *else* happened to you? Is the nanny position open now? Did Sam Calloway fire you?"

Sunny frowned. "No, he didn't fire me." Not that he hadn't thought about it. Maybe he was even still thinking about it.

"Oh," Kelly murmured, her face looking suddenly deflated. "Sam obviously is a forgiving man. That's fortunate. A woman like you probably can't afford to lose a job like that."

Sunny blinked at Kelly's words as Kim quickly came to her defense. "Just what do you mean by that? Sunny is a darn good nanny to those kids."

Kelly's pink-glossed mouth curled into a snarl. "I didn't say Sunny wasn't a good nanny. I'm just saying that Sam probably recognizes that's all she has the skills for—well, that and a theme-park princess," she said with a harsh laugh.

Mrs. Brinkman rushed over and placed her hands on Sunny's shoulders as a sign of support. "Mr. Calloway is a kind man. And smart. Smart enough to recognize and appreciate all of Sunny's wonderful qualities."

Kelly's eyebrow arched. "Does a man as rich and successful as Sam Calloway really appreciate Sunny's . . . *qualities*, or does he just pity her lack of education and skills?"

Sunny's face heated as though she'd been physically slapped. It was an undeserved low blow. Kelly knew Sunny couldn't finish her degree because she had to care for her dying grandmother. "I think you'd better leave, Kelly," she said through clenched teeth, picking up one of the cats. "You're upsetting Jo-Jo here, and I wouldn't want you to get bitten."

Kelly warily eyed the cat in Sunny's arms, then with a sniff marched out without a word.

"Sunny, I'm so sorry I told her anything," Kim said, folding her arms. "I had no idea she could be so vindictive. That woman thinks she's Paris Hilton all because she owns three cleaning stores in town. Flea was right about her. She obviously *is* after Sam."

Sunny nodded. There wasn't any doubt that Kelly had an ulterior motive for coming into the shelter. But that didn't mean Kelly didn't have a point about how ridiculous the notion of Sunny and Sam as couple would be. Sam might have kissed her, but that didn't mean he was romantically interested. What could she possibly have to offer a man as successful as Sam? He probably pitied her for being dumb enough to almost drown.

She had to get any fantasies about Sam out of her mind. It would be for the best for her to concentrate on paying off her debt. Focus more on reality.

Sam had hired her as a nanny—that was all. And from now on, a nanny was all he was going to get.

Chapter Seven

Sam thought the kids would get a kick out of visiting the animal shelter today.

True, he knew Sunny would be working there, but he wanted to take them someplace besides a park or playground. Emma and Cole loved animals. He even stopped off at the supermarket on their way over and picked up some cat and dog treats so the kids could feed them. He really didn't have any ulterior motives in mind. No preconceived purpose. He wasn't doing anything to be ashamed about. Heck, he was just doing what good fathers did for their kids nowadays!

Or at least that's what he kept telling himself.

Sam shook his head and placed his hand on the doorknob of the shelter. When he saw Sunny through the window, his breath hitched. Sunlight bounced off her straight blond hair as she stood there, smiling and cradling a black and white kitten like a baby. Sam's gut twisted, seeing her so relaxed, so happy—that same dreamy look she'd had right after he had kissed her the other day. That same look he probably had on his own face.

Face it, Calloway. You're about as transparent as this window.

All of the excuses in the world couldn't hide the fact that he was here for himself and for one purpose: to see Sunny and make sure she was okay.

"Daddy, why are we standing out here?" Cole asked, placing his hands on his hips. "Can't we just go in?"

Sam blinked at his son. "Huh? Oh. Right." He quickly put his game face on and opened the door. Emma and Cole raced over to Sunny as soon as they saw her and began cooing at the small cat she still held in her hands.

"Daddy brought us here to feed the animals," Emma announced, reaching on tiptoe to see the kitten better. "I hope they're hungry."

Sunny's face brightened as she gazed at his kids. "You know, I bet they are," she said, holding the kitten out for them to pet. She then looked over at Sam, and her expression dropped several degrees.

"Thank you for coming," she said to him. "We always appreciate donations like this."

For a rare moment in his life, Sam was left speechless. Who was this cold woman? Not Sunny. She was usually all smiles and sunshine. A trait he just realized he wanted—no, *needed*—to see today. After the drowning scare yesterday, he wanted to be around her warmth and vibrancy again. But right now, an ice cube wouldn't melt in her mouth. What had happened between yesterday and today?

"Uh, well, it's nothing," he said, finding his voice. "It was the kids' idea to come here."

Emma looked up from petting the kitten with a frown. "No, it wasn't, Daddy. It was your idea."

Heat crept up Sam's face, but he laughed off his daughter's comment with a shrug.

Kim walked out from the back room. Her brow rose when she saw Sam and the children. "Well, well, this place is sure popular today," she said with a wry grin. "Are you here to adopt an animal?"

Cole held up the bag of dog treats. "Nope. Daddy said we're only here to help feed the animals."

"Well, that's awesome. We could use the help, and I just love putting kids to work." Kim grinned as she crooked her finger, leading the children to the two back rooms where they kept the dogs and cats. "Follow me."

Sam quickly turned his attention back to Sunny, anxious to find out what was going on with her. Her shoulders were tense, and she held on to that cat like a protective shield. She cocked her head and gave the front door a longing look, as if she were thinking about bolting from his company at any second.

He quickly stepped in front of her to prevent that from happening. "Um, how are you feeling?" he asked.

"Fine."

"I've been worried about you, since you didn't want to see a doctor yesterday."

"That's kind of you." She looked down at the kitten and began running her fingers under its chin.

Sam stifled a sigh. *Conversation would be easier with that cat.* "Oh, good. I'm glad you're fine, because I was—"

"Your concern is appreciated, Mr. Calloway," she said, her tone still devoid of her usual friendliness. "You're welcome to go back with Kim and the children now, unless there was something else you wanted to discuss with me."

Mr. Calloway?

Sam's jaw tightened. That was it. He had had about enough of her businesslike attitude. "Actually, yes, Miss Fletcher," he said, playing along, "there *is* something else I'd like to discuss with you. That's so very kind of you to ask."

She nodded and politely waited for him to continue.

"I'd like to discuss why we're suddenly acting like two characters in a Jane Austen novel!" he shouted, and the devil inside him enjoyed watching her composed ruse shatter before his eyes.

The cat instantly jumped from her hands and ran from the room. *Smart cat,* he thought.

"I—I—" she stammered.

"I'm not finished yet," he growled, not caring that his temper had full reign of him. "I'd like to discuss why you wouldn't go to the hospital! I'd like to discuss why I'm addicted to your homemade brownies! I'd like to discuss how you can treat that cat with more civility than me. And I'd *really* like to discuss how you can effectively pretend we never kissed yesterday!"

Sunny's eyes widened in panic at his outrageous outburst, and she glanced over her shoulder to see if anyone had heard him. "Sam, please—"

"Oh, *now* we're back to Sam!"

"Sam, please, lower your voice," she begged. She couldn't meet his eyes, and she began to wring her hands—something he knew she did when she didn't know what to say or do—and a part of him wanted to damn near swoon with relief that he had inadvertently shocked her back to her old self. "Look, I'm sorry. I wasn't trying to be rude. I just think that maybe there should be some rules between employer and employee we should try to stick to. After what happened the other day . . . Well, I don't think it's such a good idea to *discuss* those kinds of things."

Yesterday, Sam would have wholeheartedly agreed with her. Up to a minute ago he was planning on giving her the same exact lecture. But now, after seeing her, pretending that kiss had never happened wasn't working. For him, anyway.

"You don't think we should discuss that we kissed?" he asked.

"N-no, I don't."

"Well, as your boss, I have to insist."

Sunny blinked. "Why? You're only making things difficult."

Sam rolled his eyes. *He* was the one making things difficult?

She quickly grabbed a broom and began sweeping an already clean floor. "Besides, I don't know what you want to discuss about it. Um, the kiss was . . . nice, I suppose. But believe me, you won't ever have to worry about it happening again," she said with a determined nod.

Sam folded his arms and resisted the urge to test her on that determination of hers. Sunny thought their kiss was just *nice*? *Yeah, right.* She might be full of smiles and sunshine, but she was full of something else too.

"Is that right?" he asked. "How can you be so sure it won't happen again? If memory serves me right, *I'm* the one who kissed *you.*"

She stopped sweeping and glanced up. "Oh. Right. Well, since that's the case, then you *really* don't have to worry about it happening again." She bit her lip. "Or something like that."

"Or something like that," he agreed.

She narrowed her eyes and gave him a long look before she leaned the broom back in its corner.

Sam shrugged. He was just being truthful. Sunny might be confident they'd never kiss again, but the longer he was in her presence, smelled that lemony scent of her shampoo, and was treated to those warm, sunshiny smiles of hers, the more his own confidence slipped.

Sunny dusted her hands together and wiped them on her shorts. "Well, if that's all you wanted to talk to me about, you can—"

"So this is your other job?" he asked, ignoring her hint for him to leave.

She let out an audible sigh as Sam walked over to investigate the animal cages along the back table. "Well, this is just volunteer work," she told him. "My job at the tavern starts at six tonight."

Sam frowned. "So, technically, you work *three* jobs, then? Don't you think you're spreading yourself a little thin? I mean, you almost drowned yesterday. You should give yourself a break and at least take this weekend off," he said, bending over and tapping a finger on the hamster cage.

"Don't do that!" She slapped his finger away, annoyance stamped all over her pretty face. "The hamsters are sleeping. And I don't really think it's any of your concern how thin I spread myself. What I do on my days off doesn't affect the job you've hired me to do."

He straightened and stepped away from table. Her animosity toward him and his questions about her working too much surprised him. Obviously, he'd struck a sore subject. Sunny was hiding something, and damn if he didn't want to know what it was.

"I'm sorry," he said, trying to look just that. "I'll mind my own business."

For now.

Emma came running out from the back room with Oats trotting behind. "Daddy, the kitties ate out of my hand. They're so cute. Come and see!"

"Okay," he said with chuckle. "I'll be right there."

Oats came up to Sam and nudged his hand with her nose. Her tail wagged happily as he gave her a couple of quick pats on the head, then she dropped to her belly and rolled over. *What an attention hound,* he thought with a smile. Sam hated to admit it, but Sunny's dog had grown on him.

Sunny had grown on him too.

An older woman wearing bright blue eye shadow and enough jewelry to open up a small boutique rushed through the front door waving a notebook in her wrinkled hand. "Sunny, I just talked with the Chamber of Commerce," she said, a little out of breath. The woman noticed Sam and his daughter and stopped short. "Oh, I didn't know you had . . . *visitors.*"

Sam arched an eyebrow at Sunny. He didn't know who the woman shooting him the overly animated smile was, but she seemed to know him.

"Mrs. Brinkman, this is my boss, Sam Calloway," Sunny said, making the introduction. "And his daughter, Emma."

"Oh, yes. I've seen you around town, although we haven't officially met," the woman said, holding out her heavily ringed hand to him. "I heard all about how heroic you were yesterday saving our young Sunny here."

His gaze shot to Sunny. "Heroic?" he asked, not being able to hold back a smile.

Sunny's face flushed deep pink. "Mrs. Brinkman, please,

you're exaggerating. Um, weren't you saying something about the Chamber of Commerce when you walked in?"

Mrs. Brinkman smacked her forehead with her palm. "Oh, yes, I was! Karen Curtin over at the Chamber told me she's going to call you because they want some of the animals here for the Fourth of July Parade. Isn't that great?"

"Oh, that *is* wonderful!" Sunny beamed, taking the notebook from Mrs. Brinkman. "I'll let Flea know. What great advertising! Maybe some of the pets will get adopted after the parade."

Emma tugged on Sam's hand. "Daddy, are we going to see the parade?"

"Oh, yes, you *must* see the parade!" Mrs. Brinkman exclaimed before he could answer. "It's a lovely time for everyone. People get together and picnic on the beach afterward while they wait for the fireworks. You can't miss it." She clasped her hands together and looked expectantly at Sunny. "You're going, aren't you, my dear?"

Sunny sent her a halfhearted smile. "Well . . . yes. Of course. I never miss it. You know that."

"There you go. You should go with Sam and the kids, then," Mrs. Brinkman said brightly. The woman turned and grasped Sam's arm as if to make sure he was paying close attention. "No sense in you going alone, right? Besides, Sunny's an old pro and will know the best spots to view the parade and fireworks."

Sunny rubbed her throat, looking uncomfortable at Mrs. Brinkman's not-so-subtle attempt at matchmaking. "Uh, well, Sam will probably want to spend time with his children alone. He's not going to want me hanging around on his day off."

"Sure he will!" Emma blurted. "We want you to show us where all the best spots are for the parade. Isn't that right, Daddy?"

Sam sent Sunny a helpless shrug, not exactly disappointed with the way his Fourth of July holiday was shaping up. Maybe it was wrong to want to explore the attraction he had for Sunny, but it wouldn't hurt to get to know the woman he'd hired to watch his children a little better at the very least. "I guess you're stuck with us," he told Sunny, grinning.

"Oh, boy! Wait till I tell Cole," Emma exclaimed as she ran off.

Mrs. Brinkman smiled and let out a contented sigh. "Well, I'd better go back to my store now. So nice meeting you, Mr. Calloway."

"Call me, Sam, please."

"Sam." Her eyes twinkled mischievously. "Sam and Sunny. Yes, I like that. You must bring your children by my store when you're done visiting here. I give out pretzel rods to all the children I like."

"You give out pretzel rods to all the children you *don't* like too," Sunny said dryly.

Mrs. Brinkman waved off Sunny's comment. "I'm just two doors down," she told Sam. "Don't forget to stop by, dear."

"I won't forget, Mrs. Brinkman. Thank you."

As soon as the older woman was out the door, Sunny walked over and laid a hand on his arm. "Sam, are you sure you want me tagging along to the parade with you and the children? I mean, it may not be a good idea. I could easily come up with an excuse to back out."

Sam's gaze dropped to his forearm, where Sunny's hand

still lingered. The warmth from her fingers felt like a heating pad, spreading throughout his body until even his throat went hot and dry.

It was on the tip of his tongue to back out of going to the parade with her. Despite his attraction, he still had some reservations about her. But then his gaze met hers, and when he saw real concern in her striking blue eyes, he wondered how he'd ever thought this woman was like all the others in his past.

"No, I don't want you to back out," he said truthfully. "Besides, we wouldn't want to disappoint Emma and Cole, right?"

She cocked her head as if to think it over. "I guess you're right. It'll be fun." She finally let out a smile, that warm and wonderful smile he'd been taking for granted since he'd first met her, and for a brief moment he thought about chucking those proper employer-employee rules of hers right then and there and taking her into his arms.

His cell phone went off. It was just the ice cube down the back he needed. He checked the number. Mark was trying to get ahold of him on a Saturday. Again. What the heck couldn't wait until Monday?

He looked at Sunny, about to explain that he needed to take the call, but she had already turned away, blocking him out by busying herself with the hamsters and straightening up around them.

Well . . . good, he thought. There was no need for any lengthy discussion about their parade plans. That could all be sorted out next week. At least Sunny was acting like herself again, and everything was back to normal. It's not like he wanted one of her dazzling smiles pointed at him for one second longer than necessary anyway. Right?

He sighed as he brought the phone up to his ear. *Focus, Sam.*

Normally, a call on his day off wouldn't faze him in the least. This was the kind of life he was looking for when he and Mark decided to create their company. A few years ago he'd desperately needed to throw himself into something after Kate left, to focus on something else besides what a pitiful fool he'd been in thinking his wife had loved him for *him* and not what he could do for her. Work was the perfect solution to the emotional struggles he'd been dealing with— better than anything else he could use to escape reality or escape . . . *feeling.* Perhaps, because of that, he had never minded the minor interruptions work brought to his personal life.

But for some reason, today the intrusion damn well irritated him.

Chapter Eight

On Monday evening, Sunny wanted a long soak in her tub. She could have just kicked herself for ever complaining about her short-lived princess job on the boardwalk *or* her aching feet while she had worked there. Waitressing at the Blowfish Tavern proved to be far more challenging than she'd anticipated, especially since the summer tourist season was at its height and business had doubled.

She had reported bright and early for work this morning at Sam's and quickly learned his kids wanted to go on a tour of the ocean museum. She didn't think she had the energy, but the children's enthusiasm over such simple things as seashells was infectious. More important, it was a great excuse to get out of the house and away from their father. Her infatuation with Sam was becoming a distraction, and now she worried whether it was such a great idea to spend the Fourth of July holiday with him.

Sunny walked into her house and gingerly sank into her favorite recliner. Oats automatically came prancing over to her and laid her nose on Sunny's lap.

"I know, girl," she murmured, lightly stroking her dog's head. "I missed you too. What's the matter, not getting enough attention nowadays?" Oats let out a long moan in response.

Sunny tilted her head back and closed her eyes, willfully ignoring the aches in her legs. So this was what life has become? Alone, overworked, and holding conversations with her dog? Maybe Sam had a point. Maybe she *was* spreading herself a little too thin among her jobs. The fact that she had already resigned herself to sleeping in this chair tonight told her Sam might even have *more* than just a mere point. But if she wanted to keep up with her bills, what choice did she really have?

A knock sounded at the door. Oats let out a loud *woof* and ran to the front of the house to investigate. Sunny sank farther into the cushions and hoped whoever it was would go away.

The last thing she thought she could do right now was move.

The doorbell rang next. Oats came running back into the living room, barking and circling the room from the musical chimes. Obviously, whoever it was was *not* going to go away. She reluctantly pushed herself out of the chair.

When she answered the door, she was greeted with Flea's friendly face. "Hi, Sunny," he said with a shy grin. "I hope I'm not disturbing you."

She had to smile. Flea wore a red Phillies baseball cap and stood eagerly holding his briefcase in front of him with both hands, adding to his already boyish manner. "Not at all," she lied, stepping aside to let him in. "Come on. I'll pour us some lemonade." She headed toward the kitchen, and he followed, shuffling his sneakers on the hardwood floor behind her.

She pulled out a pitcher of lemonade from the refrigerator

and set it on the counter. As she reached for a couple of glasses, she asked, "So, to what do I owe this unexpected visit?"

"I have something I want to give you."

Sunny's thoughts immediately went to what Kim had said last week about Flea having a crush on her, and her eyes widened in panic. She whirled around. "I can't accept it," she blurted, hugging the glasses to her chest for support.

Flea blinked. "What do you mean you can't accept it? You don't even know what *it* is yet."

"It—it doesn't matter. I think it's best you not give me what you have there. I don't want anything affecting our friendship."

Flea squinted at her. "Sunny, what are you talking about? What I have here isn't going to affect our friendship."

She set down the glasses and looked at him warily. "It's not?"

"Of course not. You know, you haven't been yourself ever since you started working for that Sam Calloway."

Tell me about it.

Her shoulders sank as she let out a deep, relieved breath. Flea was right on the money with that comment. She hadn't been acting like herself at all. And she knew why. There was no use denying it any longer. She had developed feelings for Sam.

"Are you okay?" Flea asked.

She had a crush on her boss, was currently in a financial mess, and talked to her dog more frequently than would be socially accepted. No, she was far from okay.

"Um, yeah, I'm fine." She shook her head and sighed. "I'm sorry. What did you want to give me?"

"Well, actually, it's something I've wanted to discuss with

you for a while." He snapped open his briefcase and pulled out a stack of papers, laying them out neatly in front of her. "What do you think about becoming a veterinarian?"

Sunny blinked at the papers and then at Flea. *Become a veterinarian?*

"I can't do that," she protested, shoving the papers away. Amusement suddenly bubbled up inside her, and she gave in to a laugh at the sheer ridiculousness of his suggestion. Flea might as well have suggested she become an astronaut. Both were vocations far out of her galaxy.

"Of course you can," Flea said, frowning, pushing the papers back in front of her. "I've seen you with the animals, Sunny. I know you love working with them. You're smart and have a sixth sense when it comes to judging their needs. Sea Bright College of Medicine and Science now offers classes. It would be a thirty-minute commute for you. I even brought you a list of scholarships you could apply for."

Sunny bit her lip. The idea did sound strangely tempting. She'd always regretted not going back to school. But everything was so complicated now. With her working two jobs, she didn't see how she'd ever have the time. Plus, what if she couldn't handle the curriculum?

"I—I don't know, Flea," she said, feeling overwhelmed at the thought of such a huge undertaking, "maybe that's something I can consider doing in the future. I'm not sure it's the time."

He shot her a disappointed look. "Oh, come on. If you don't do this now, you'll never do it."

She started to shake her head, but Flea walked over to her and placed both hands on her shoulders, willing her to look him in the eye. "Listen, you *can* do it. I didn't want to mention this, but I heard about what Kelly said to you last week . . . about your not having skills."

Shame washed over her, and she looked away. What Kelly had said had hurt her feelings, and although it still stung, it was also the truth. She didn't have any skills. She could baby-sit and wait tables. But even the waiting tables part was iffy.

As if reading her mind, Flea gave her a little shake. "She was wrong, Sunny. You *do* have skills, and you have the capacity to have even more. You need to do this for yourself. This year. If you ever want to be able to stand on your own two feet again and stop working these crazy jobs and schedules, then you need to make a career decision and work toward it."

"But what if it's totally over my head?"

"It won't be. Stop running from things that you think are too difficult."

She shot a hand to her hip. "Hey, since when do I run from things that are too difficult?"

"I *could* mention the swimming thing," he said, his voice thick with good humor.

"Well, for your information, I *will* be taking swim lessons, smarty-pants. Starting next weekend."

Flea's eyebrows shot up. "Hey, that's great," he said with a grin. "I'm so proud of you. Where are you going to take them? At the Aquatic Center in town?"

Her cheeks heated. Knowing how Flea felt about Sam, she knew her answer wasn't going to go over too well with him. She bit the inside of her cheek, stalling for time. "Oh, well, no. Uh, Sam Calloway said he would teach me."

"Oh." Flea's mouth turned hard, and he dropped his arms. "What a prince," he muttered.

"What do you mean by that?"

"Rich business moguls like Sam Calloway do not merely decide to do things like that without a price, if you know what I mean."

Sunny couldn't help it; she burst into laughter. And if Flea knew anything about Sam, he would laugh too. Until recently Sam had avoided her like the plague. And even though he had kissed her, Sam definitely didn't strike her as the womanizer type.

Flea's brow furrowed. "I wouldn't laugh. Do you have any idea who his wife was, Sunny?" He paused a beat. "Kate Bovier."

Sunny instantly sobered, and her eyes widened. *Kate Bovier?* Kate Bovier had done modeling for the *Victoria's Secret* catalog, along with some TV commercial work, although most of her publicity had come from tabloid magazines due to her excessive partying. Eventually her lifestyle had caught up to her, and she died of a drug overdose at a Los Angeles nightclub a few years back. Sunny had no idea the model was even married, let alone a mother of two small children.

"Oh" was all she could say.

"Yeah, 'oh,'" Flea repeated. "Sam Calloway isn't the great white knight you're looking for, Sunny. He obviously has a penchant for beautiful, wild women."

Sunny frowned. She refused to believe something like that. That seemed so unlike the Sam she knew. So unlike the man she saw in him when he was with his children. "You're not being fair to Sam," she told him.

Flea's expression softened. "Yeah, you're right," he said with a sad smile. "*Correction.* The man now seems to have a penchant for beautiful women with kind hearts." He gave her a gentle finger tap on her nose, then snapped his briefcase closed and turned away. "Just be careful with him, Sunny."

She *had* been careful. It wasn't like Kim hadn't warned her too. For all the good it had done. It wasn't like she *wanted* to have feelings for Sam. She knew the man was out of her league. It had just sort of . . . happened.

Flea grabbed his briefcase and headed for the door. About to leave, he stopped himself and gave her a long look. "Sunny, you're in a vulnerable state right now—financially and emotionally. Promise me you'll think about what I said about school—*and* about Sam."

She nodded, even though she didn't need to make that promise. She had a sneaky suspicion she wasn't going to think of anything else for the rest of the night.

"I love the parade!" Emma shouted over the noise of the crowd.

Cole grinned and waved his tiny American flag over his head. "I wish we could have a parade like this every day!"

Sunny laughed. Despite her initial reservations, she was enjoying her decision to spend the Fourth of July holiday with Sam and the kids. It was almost as if she and Sam and the children were a real family today. That lonely ache she'd been carrying around in her heart since her grandmother's passing had lifted, and she wanted to hold on to this day for as long as she could.

However, she couldn't shake what Flea had told her about Sam's wife. She just couldn't wrap her mind around Sam being married to such a flamboyant party girl as Kate Bovier. Sam seemed so down-to-earth and responsible. But Sunny knew firsthand what it was like to have people spread gossip about you, so she was willing to reserve judgment on Sam's wife until she could ask him about his marriage.

Sunny snuck a peek at Sam just then. He was bouncing his daughter on his lap and waving to Smokey the Bear. She bit down on a laugh and averted her eyes. It was so nice to see Sam having fun. In fact, this was the first time Sam had actually seemed relaxed and less guarded since she'd met him—he wasn't even checking his BlackBerry every two seconds. She never did have that talk with Sam about his workaholic ways. It was just as well. Apparently those concerns she'd had were unwarranted.

The parade finally ended, and people were filling the street and walking to their various destinations. Sam slid off the stone wall he'd been sitting on and chuckled as he dropped Emma to her feet. "Well, I'm going to go out on a limb and declare the parade a hit," he said dryly. He looked at Sunny. "So where to now, boss?"

Her eyes connected with Sam's, and those initial concerns she'd felt about spending time with him outside of work all came flooding back—along with about a hundred butterflies in her stomach. He was so bone-meltingly handsome in his baby blue polo shirt and denim cargo shorts. Casual was a good look for him—although she suspected *anything* was probably a good look for him. Sam smelled nice too, which had made it doubly hard to concentrate during the parade. Every so often, when he'd leaned in to speak to her over the noise of the crowd, she'd caught tiny waves of his fresh-scented aftershave and had to resist the urge to melt into the poor man's lap.

Sunny stepped back to clear her mind. "How about we—"

Sam's cell phone suddenly went off. She frowned as he pulled it out of his shorts pocket and glanced at the number.

"Sorry, but I should take this," he murmured.

Sunny looked at the disappointed expressions on his children's faces. They didn't want their fun day to be interrupted any more than she did.

She covered Sam's phone with her hand. "Do you really need to?" she asked in a hushed tone. "I mean, it's a holiday, after all. Can't it wait until tomorrow?"

"I'm afraid not. It's important."

Aren't Cole and Emma more important?

Sunny glanced at the children again. Their sad little upturned faces staring back at her nearly broke her heart. She didn't think then. She just reacted.

"Hey!" Sam yelled as she ripped the phone from his hand and sent it sailing into the street. To her horror, it bounced twice with loud crunches, then smashed into several pieces. She froze as laughter and shouts rapidly came from onlookers.

Before Sunny could register what she had actually done, Sam was in her face. "Are you nuts?" he shouted. "Have you completely lost it? Why would you do something like that?"

She forgot to breathe as she stared into Sam's storm-filled eyes. She had had so many reasons as to why she had thrown his phone away—mainly because Emma and Cole deserved his attention—but it wasn't the time to go into a lengthy diatribe of her opinion of his work habits. All she could do now was apologize for her temper and defuse the situation.

"I—I'm sorry, Sam."

"Whoa, cool," Cole said in awe. "I wish I could have done that. Daddy, can I go look at your phone?"

Sam blinked down at his son. "What? No, you may not go look at it. And cell phones are not to be thrown around like softballs, despite what your nanny just demonstrated."

Sunny thought for sure that Sam would fire her on the

spot. The fact that he still referred to her as *your nanny* filled her with a dizzying relief that she still had her job. But by not calling her by name, Sam was sending her another message: she'd crossed the line. And it worried her to think she might have jeopardized their growing friendship by her rash action.

Emma walked over to Sam and hugged his legs. "Daddy, don't feel bad. I didn't like that dumb old phone anyway."

"You didn't?" he murmured, staring dumbfounded at what used to be his very expensive phone.

She shook her head. "No, it was stupid. I'm glad it's dead."

"Me too," echoed Cole. "You liked it more than you liked us."

Sam whipped his head toward his children and frowned. "Hey, that's not true," he said fiercely, bending down to their level. "I love you guys. You mean more to me than any old phone—or anything. *Always* remember that."

Tears stung Sunny's eyes as Sam and his children shared a group hug. Thank goodness Sam now knew how his children felt about his work habits. Maybe her actions were rash, but she was sure Sam would see that the outcome was worth it. She let out a little relieved sigh.

Sam pinned her with his gaze. "This doesn't mean you're off the hook," he said with a scowl.

She gulped. "Oh. But—but I'm really sorry, Sam."

"Yeah, I got that part." He stood and rubbed his face, frustration still etched in his forehead.

"Look, how about we all cool off with some ice cream?" she suggested, hoping to divert the situation. "Maybe we can get some and take it down to the beach while we wait for the fireworks to start."

"Yay! Ice cream!" his children cried.

Oats let out a few yelps along with them. Sunny laughed. "Sorry, no ice cream for you, girl," she said, patting her dog's head.

Sam shook his head and treated her to one of his rare smiles. Those butterflies in her stomach returned, right on cue. "Okay, you're off the hook *for now*. Lead the way," he said, gesturing to the sidewalk.

They silently walked together, passing Mrs. Brinkman's clothing store and the animal shelter. As soon as the kids saw the giant sign for Double Dips Ice Cream Parlor, they ran ahead and through the door.

"You go catch up with them," she told Sam. "I'll be right there. I can't bring Oats into the store, so I'm just going to tie her up out here while we get our ice cream."

Sam nodded and followed his children into the store. Sunny spotted a shade tree and knelt down to begin tying Oats' leash to it.

"Well, well, if this isn't a sight for sore eyes," said a slurred male voice. "Nothing brings a smile to my face quicker than a beautiful woman on her knees."

Kenny Twardski's mocking tone made Sunny clench her teeth until they hurt. Her day, which had started out so lovely, was getting worse and worse. But she refused to let Kenny get to her.

She slowly stood and gazed up at the man's sun-beaten face. "Kenny, I feel it is my duty to inform you that any connection between *your* reality and *mine* is purely coincidental." She tried to step past him, but he grabbed hold of her arm.

"Now, honey, you know I'm just teasing," he said, giving her a lazy grin. "Why do you always have to get all huffy with me?"

She stared at him, anger competing with annoyance. "Well, I'll try being nicer if you'll try being smarter."

His smug smile faltered, then widened. "Well, you weren't so smart getting yourself into that debt of yours, now, were you?"

That did it! Mentioning her financial problems was a low blow. She wasn't going to waste one more minute in this jerk's presence. She tried to yank her arm out of his grasp, but his fingers squeezed tighter. "Ow! Kenny, let go."

Instead, he roughly tugged her closer, forcing her to brace her palm on his chest to keep from falling into him. She shivered in the summer heat as his fingers dug into her arm. His peeling, sunburned nose and the smell of beer on his breath only added to her disgust.

"If you're still having money problems, I can talk to my dad," he said in a more intimate tone. "He'll hire you back in a second if you—"

A firm hand landed squarely on Kenny's shoulder, breaking off the rest of his words. "Is there a problem?" Sam asked, directing his question at Sunny.

Sunny angled her head to address Sam, and her eyes widened. The line of his mouth was flat, and the look in his eyes was about as cold as a shark's. Sam usually had a somewhat intimidating manner about him—especially when he was yelling at her—but right then and there he looked downright bloodthirsty.

Hoping to avoid a scene, Sunny gave him a reassuring smile. "Everything's fine, Sam."

Kenny immediately let go of her arm and backed away a few steps. "Yeah, no problem here," he told Sam. Kenny stole a glance at Sunny, shooting her a grin that held no humor. "Just saying hi to an old friend."

Sam's voice turned as cold as his gaze. "Well, now it's time to say good-bye, *old friend.*"

Kenny puffed out his chest and sized up Sam. Probably coming to the conclusion that he was outmatched in size and strength, he nodded. "Yeah, all right. Bye, Sunny. Don't be a stranger," he added, turning and walking away.

After Kenny disappeared down the street, Sam folded his arms, his face looking even more tense. "Who the hell was that?"

"Nobody," she said tersely, checking her arm for bruises. *Nobody but an idiot*, she wanted to add. Fortunately, her arm was fine. Lucky for Kenny. She glanced up and looked beyond Sam. "Hey, where are the children?" she asked.

"They're inside eating their ice cream. We were waiting for you, then I decided to come out and see what was taking so long, and I saw . . . Look, are you okay?"

She managed a smile, even though she was embarrassed that Sam had had to come to her rescue. Again. First he had to fish her out of the bay, and now this. It was almost becoming a regular job—being her personal knight in shining armor—and one she was afraid she could get used to rather easily.

"I'm fine, Sam. Kenny was just a little tipsy. That's all. Combine that with his regular jerkiness, and you get that kind of melodramatic nonsense."

The funny thing was that in all the years she'd known Kenny, this was the first time he had actually laid a hand on her. Not that she was scared of him or anything, especially since they were out in public. Kenny might have had a few beers during the parade, but essentially the situation was harmless, despite how it had probably looked to Sam.

Sam gently took hold of both her shoulders and dipped his head to meet her eyes. "Are you sure you're okay? Tipsy or not, I didn't like the way that guy was looking at you."

She cocked her head and studied him for a moment. If she didn't know better, she'd think Sam was actually jealous. Jealous of a weasel like Kenny Twardski? The thought made her giddy, and she wanted to grin from ear to ear, but she carefully kept her expression blank as she gazed back into his serious eyes. "You didn't like how he was looking at me?" she repeated.

He slowly shook his head, keeping his eyes fixed on hers. "No, I didn't. I, uh, didn't like the way he was touching you either."

Her face heated, but she knew it wasn't from standing out in the sun all this time. The way Sam was looking at her made her feel all warm and gooey inside. "Like the way you're touching me now?" she murmured with a smile.

"Yeah," he breathed. His fingers tightened on her shoulders, and he leaned in, looking as though he would kiss her. But when she tilted her chin up, he quickly frowned and, with the same amount of abruptness, dropped his arms.

"Uh, the kids are waiting for us," he said, gesturing behind him with his thumb.

"Oh, of course," she said, trying to keep the disappointment out of her voice. She lowered her gaze and began brushing imaginary lint off her shorts.

Gosh, she was such an idiot! What had she really expected, that Sam was going to kiss her again or maybe decide out of the blue that they should date? *Dumb. Dumb. Dumb.*

"Sunny," he said, causing her to glance up. "I . . ." Sam's

eyes were suddenly full of warmth and tenderness and maybe a little . . . *regret?* Then he looked away and over her shoulder. "You look like you need an ice cream."

"Ice cream?" she choked. Right at that moment, ice cream was the dead last thing she needed—or wanted.

"Yeah." He shrugged a shoulder. "My treat."

She laughed, in spite of how emotionally fragile she felt. Sam was holding back from her. She felt it. She saw it in his eyes, in his stance. He wouldn't admit they'd shared a connection just then, and her heart sank. Did he not want to get involved with a woman who would never fit into his rich, corporate world? It seemed like a perfectly reasonable reservation to have from someone like Sam, who probably prided himself on his self-made success. She was still struggling to fit into her ex-amusement-park-princess world. And doing a damn poor job of it.

Sunny had to face the facts. She wasn't much of a catch for anyone, considering the current financial mess her life was in. If Sam was offering her just ice cream, she would have to take it. She doubted she could get a better offer.

"Two scoops with rainbow sprinkles?" she asked, trying to sound upbeat.

A dry smile kicked up the corners of his mouth as he led her into the ice cream parlor. "Somehow, I knew you were a rainbow sprinkles kind of woman."

Chapter Nine

Sunny glanced over her shoulder and saw that Emma and
Cole had fallen asleep on the ride home from the fireworks.
She wasn't surprised. By the time Sam had maneuvered
though all the traffic and pulled up to his house, it was well
past ten o'clock.

She and Sam shared a smile as they quietly slipped out of
the car. Sam picked up Cole and gently shifted him over his
shoulder as Sunny lifted Emma out of the car. She followed
Sam into the house and up the steps, being careful not to
wake either of the children.

Once upstairs, Sam wedged open the door of Cole's bed-
room with his foot and disappeared into the dark room.
Sunny made her way a little farther down the hall into
Emma's bedroom, then gently laid her on the bed.

As soon as Emma's head hit the pillow, she stirred, and
her eyelids fluttered open. "I had the best day," she whispered
sleepily.

"I'm so glad." Sunny smiled and took a seat on the edge
of the bed. Spending the holiday with Sam and the children

had been one of the best days she'd had in a long time too. Sunny had forgotten all about the money problems hanging over her head. More important, she'd managed to forget how lonely she'd been since her grandmother died.

"What was your favorite part?" Sunny asked softly, stroking the girl's head. "The fireworks or the parade?"

"The part when you threw Daddy's phone into the street and it blew up into a million trillion pieces."

Sunny rolled her eyes. "I had a feeling you were going to say that. At least that phone never knew what hit it."

Emma giggled, then let out a huge yawn. Taking that as a signal that she should leave, Sunny instinctively bent over and kissed her on her forehead. The child's face lit up at that simple token of affection, and tenderness washed over Sunny. Such a reaction by Emma struck her as unusual, and she couldn't help but wonder if Emma remembered ever getting a good-night kiss from her real mother.

Her chest grew heavy at the thought that maybe Emma didn't.

"You'd better get some sleep," Sunny said, blinking back her tears and tucking the child in with a pink and green comforter. "Nighty-night."

Before Sunny could slip out of the room, Emma fell back asleep.

Sam was already sitting at the kitchen table when Sunny came back downstairs. As soon as she took in his face, she hesitated by the steps. He was perfectly still, staring at the floor, all but drilling holes into the hardwood with his eyes. His expression was hard and his jaw tensed to an almost perfect right angle. Whatever was going through Sam's mind at that moment didn't seem pleasant. She wanted to leave him alone with those thoughts, but her traitorous dog was lying by his feet, ignoring her silent command to come to her.

"Um, Emma's in bed," she said quietly, "so I guess I'll get Oats and be on my—"

Sam's head whipped up. "Wait. I want to talk to you."

Sunny tensed but kept her voice nonchalant. "Oh? About what?"

"I think you know."

Her shoulders drooped. *Wonderful.* Of course she knew what Sam wanted to talk about. But part of her had hoped Sam had forgiven and forgotten all about the jihad she waged on his cell phone earlier this afternoon.

"Well, okay. Go ahead." She nodded but remained standing where she was.

He waited several beats. Then his lips twitched. "Sunny, it would be easier to talk if we were at least in the same room together."

"Oh. Right." She rushed over to him, determined to state her case and change his opinion of her. "Sam, I don't know what came over me. I was just so . . . so . . . You have to believe that I've never thrown away *anyone's* phone before in my entire life."

"Well, I'm honored you decided to begin this anger-management plan with *my* phone."

She shrugged helplessly. "I had to get your attention somehow. It was the only—"

He raised his hand in a calming gesture. "Let's just say mission accomplished and leave it at that."

She blew out a sigh of relief when she saw the amusement in his eyes. Although she didn't fool herself into thinking that meant he truly forgave her. "I really am sorry, Sam."

Sam leaned forward, pinching the bridge of his nose.

"Look, don't worry. I'm over it. Actually, based on how my children reacted today, your phone-pitching served as an overdue wake-up call for me. It's made me do some thinking." He dropped his hand and looked up, the expression in his eyes so heartbreaking that tears began to form in her own. "I've come to the conclusion that I've been very blind and very selfish lately."

Sunny couldn't exactly disagree with his assessment, but she also couldn't allow him to shoulder the responsibility alone. She sank into the chair opposite him. "Sam, I feel partly to blame for this mess. I've wanted to talk to you about your work habits and how they've been affecting the kids for some time. I'm sorry. I should have said something to you sooner."

He hung his head, rubbing his forehead as if his head hurt. "I'm not sure how receptive I would have been."

It disturbed her to see such an imposing man as Sam look so broken and helpless. She wanted so badly to reach out and touch him, to comfort him, but she was afraid he might close up on her. So she simply waited with her hands in her lap until he was ready to say more.

"It's hard to accept, you know," he said with a humorless chuckle.

"Hard to accept . . . what?"

Sam's voice fell shockingly soft as he lifted his gaze back up to hers. "That my kids love me for *me*."

She blinked, almost unsure she'd heard him right. She couldn't imagine *anyone* not loving Sam for exactly who he was, especially his own children. How could he think otherwise? The idea made her feel sick. "Well, of course, they do! Why else would they love you?"

He shrugged. "I don't know. Maybe I'm just not used to

people wanting to be around me without having a hidden motive or agenda."

Sunny listened in bewilderment. What an awful thing to believe. She wished she could convince him otherwise. She couldn't imagine always having to wonder if people really wanted to be around him just because of his money and connections. No wonder he always seemed so sad and was so afraid to trust her. Apparently Sam had decided to take that guesswork out of his life by making himself appear cold and unlikeable to people in order to guard his feelings. But she had seen through his façade early on. She knew there was more to Sam deep down inside, and she wanted to know even more, so the question "Is that why you and your wife divorced?" slipped out before she could stop herself from asking.

He snorted. "Among other reasons. But, yes, Kate wasn't exactly the person I thought she was. It turned out she loved my money and what she could do with it more than she loved me *or* the children."

"I'm so sorry, Sam." She knew the words were lacking as soon as they left her mouth, but it was all she had to offer. All that he would *let* her offer.

He shook his head. "The kids never knew—thank God—so they took her death pretty hard. Their behavior at school and with the other nanny started to become challenging, so I came here because I thought Emma and Cole could use a change of scenery. I thought it would help them heal. It seemed like the perfect plan at the time." He let out a wry grin. "But as you pointed out in your, uh, unorthodox way, they didn't need a different town. What they really need is *me*."

I need you too, she wanted to add. But she couldn't. Her

instincts told her she couldn't tell him that no matter how much she wanted to. Sam obviously still bore emotional scars from his past, and she couldn't have him thinking she needed him because of her own money problems. He'd probably think she was no better than Kate.

She cleared her throat. "Well, I'm glad you realize that. I know firsthand how it feels to come in second. I just didn't want to see you making that mistake with Emma and Cole."

Sam's gray eyes narrowed and bored into her. "What do you mean, you know how it feels?"

Her fingers flew to her mouth. She hadn't intended to share this much with him. She had never spoken about her father to anyone except her grandmother. But her guard always seemed to be down around Sam. He was just so easy to be with and talk to. It was just as effortless as listening to him.

"Um, do you think Oats needs to be let out?" she asked, deciding to direct his attention elsewhere.

"Uh-uh," Sam said, shaking his finger at her. "Oats is fine. Answer the question. You opened the door. Now you have to walk through it. Tell me what you meant."

She smiled in spite of herself. Sam had opened up to her; she supposed it only right to reciprocate—no matter how painful it was for her to talk about. But she had a feeling he needed to hear it now.

"Okay. Fair enough." She dropped her gaze to her hands and let a few moments pass while she thought about it. "When I said I know how it feels to come in second, I meant that I was never the number one priority in my father's life. My father didn't put a career first, but he did choose something else over me. Mom-mom told me he couldn't handle my mother's death, so he turned to alcohol to cope.

That's why she ended up raising me. When my father drank, everything else around him seem to suffer: the house, his job—"

"You?" Sam finished, searching her face. "And did *you* suffer as well?"

Her cheeks heated, and she ducked her head to keep him from noticing. "Well, I was just a baby at the time, so I don't really remember all of it. But, yes, it hurts to know I was so easily forgotten about, so easily left. I guess I still wish things had turned out differently."

He placed his fingertip underneath her chin, tilting her head up until their eyes met. "You look like you turned out pretty well to me," he said with a gentle smile.

As she gazed into his eyes, that last little part of her resistance toward him slipped away. Sam didn't show his compassionate side often, but when he did, it had the ability to wreak havoc with her insides, particularly her heart. Why did he have to be so kind and look so good? She was in dangerous territory, and if she didn't walk—no, *run*—away from him right now, she might not ever.

Luckily, she was an expert "runner." Most of her life had been spent running away from difficult situations—her water fears, going back to college. She was trying to face them now, though. All except one fear.

The fear that she had fallen in love with Sam.

She grabbed Oats' leash and stood. "It's late. I'd better go."

Without another word, she made a mad dash to exit, almost tripping over her own dog in the process. Sam probably thought she was a madwoman taking off like that, but she didn't care.

Swinging open the front door, she was hit by the salty, muggy scent of the evening bay air. She breathed it in hard to clear her senses. Unfortunately, the scent of Sam was still strong in her mind; otherwise she would have been grateful for the reprieve.

She hopped down the porch steps and figured she was home free, but almost out of nowhere, Sam reached out and caught her hand.

"Hey, what's your rush?" he asked, his eyes wide with concern. "Did I say something wrong back there?"

She almost laughed at that. Little did he know, he didn't say or do anything wrong. Sam was perfect. She was the inexperienced one. The one who was second best. It was all her. Her problem. Her inability to control her feelings for him whenever they were together. Even now, as he stood frowning at her, worried that he had done something to cause her to bolt out of his house, she wanted to throw her arms around him and never let go.

With a little sigh, she gently pulled her hand out of his and tucked it into her shorts pocket. "You didn't say anything wrong, Sam. I—I just have to leave now."

"Just like that? Without saying good-bye?"

"Good-bye."

She didn't turn around and walk away, though. Sam made no effort to move either. She *wanted* to walk away. Sam probably already thought she was crazy, and the best thing she could do for her self-respect was to leave now.

Move, feet! Move!

But she just stood there. Her mouth and mind were in agreement, but her legs obviously had a will of their own. Oats must have picked up on that vibe too, because her dog made the sudden decision to drop to the grass with a grunt and sprawl out on her tummy.

Sam glanced at her dog, looking slightly relieved. Sunny was about to try the good-bye thing all over again, but he suddenly reached out and took a strand of her hair between his fingertips.

He grinned as he inspected it. "You have rainbow sprinkles in your hair."

Mesmerized by his touch and the heady look in his eyes, she felt as if her lungs were being wrung out of every last drop of air. "Oh, do I?" she managed.

Her voice sounded so wispy to her own ears, she wasn't sure he had even heard her, but then his grin widened. He leaned in and was so close to her, his belt buckle clinked with the zipper on her sweater.

"I can take them out for you," he whispered against the side of her mouth.

A little thrill crept up her spine. Her tongue felt too thick and clumsy to speak, and she was so paralyzed by having Sam's lips so close to hers, she couldn't even nod. If it wasn't for her heart beating like a heavy metal drum, Sam probably would have had to check her for a pulse. Automatically, her gaze turned to his mouth, and that's when she knew he was going to kiss her.

She wasn't wrong. In an instant Sam's lips were on hers, and she clung to him, kissing him right back. There was no gentle exploration of her mouth or any amount of uncertainty conveyed in his touch this time. He was rough and forceful. Demanding. Excitement coursed through her as he tugged her even closer, pressing his hips against hers. Sam wasn't a game-player. He wanted her, and he was making sure she knew it.

She half moaned into his mouth, her hands winding their

way through his soft, wavy hair. She wanted him too. So badly. And just when she thought her body would go up in smoke, Sam pulled back slightly.

His lips quirked, but the expression in his eyes was still full of desire. "You know, I'm not normally in the habit of kissing my employees."

She had to laugh. "That's good, because I'm not normally in the habit of kissing my employers."

"Well, would you like to make it a habit—with me?" He cleared his throat. "You know, for the summer?"

For the summer . . .

She froze. The night was silent, but those three little words reverberated like cymbals crashing together in her head. Those words also stung more than any possible rejection Sam could have given her instead.

She lowered her gaze and slowly drew out of his arms. What a dope she was. She actually believed this was the beginning of her happily-ever-after. Her fairy-tale romance. But here Sam was already putting in the stop-order to the time they would be spending together.

"Sunny," he said gently. But she wouldn't look at him yet. She was afraid her face would betray her thoughts.

He dipped his head to meet her eyes. "Hey. I just want to make sure you know I'm in."

She blinked, then frowned. "You're in? Did you step in something?" she asked, looking down and inspecting his feet. "I thought I did a good job cleaning up after Oats."

He chuckled. "No, no, I'm not standing in anything." He lifted her chin back up with his index finger. "I'm trying to tell you that I'm *in* to what's going on between us."

"Oh . . ." she said, trying to process what he was telling

her. Sam was in to giving in to their attraction, but nothing more. She obviously wasn't good enough for a regular relationship. And he didn't love her.

Or at least not like she loved him.

Sam probably thought his announcement was a major breakthrough in his psyche, but she couldn't exactly be glad for him. In fact, his little declaration only sank her into depression.

He stroked her cheek with his thumb. "Hey, what's the matter? I thought you'd be happy."

Happy? She would have laughed if she wasn't afraid she'd cry if she moved even one cheek muscle. So much for fairy-tale relationships. She wanted to sue Disney for getting her hopes up like this. Out of all the princess movies she had ever seen, not one of them had ever had a happily-ever-after that concluded with the prince telling the princess, "I'm in."

"Isn't this what you want too?" Sam asked, his eyes growing wide when she just stood there in silence.

No. Not at all. She wanted much more—a husband, a family. The kind of family she didn't have growing up. The whole nine yards. Instead, Sam offered her just a taste of it. For the summer only.

Could she be satisfied with something so wonderful for such a short amount of time? Could she handle coming in second in another man's life?

Sam had feelings for her that went beyond mere attraction. She knew it deep down inside. But she also knew Sam wasn't the type to rush into any kind of declaration of love, especially after everything he'd been through with his ex-wife. She'd have to be patient with him if she ever hoped to have it all with him.

Sensing his concern, she gave him a weak smile. "Nothing's wrong. I was just thinking about the children," she lied. "What will you tell them? I mean, about us?"

Sam rubbed his chin. "Well, nothing. For now. I'd like to keep our relationship professional around them for the most part. I guess we'll just play it by ear," he said, drawing her into his arms again.

She closed her eyes and drew in a deep breath. *Patience, Sunny. Patience.*

Sam began nuzzling her neck, and the tenseness of their conversation diffused from her body. She wrapped her arms around him to keep her legs from giving way. If this went on much longer, the neighbors might call the police.

"I should go, Sam," she said with a sigh.

"Yeah, I suppose so," he murmured against her skin. Then he lifted his head and began kissing the other side of her neck.

She chuckled. "You're making things difficult again."

"I'm a difficult man."

Sam *was* a difficult man. No doubt about that. But he purposely made himself so. Was he giving her some sort of a warning about that?

Sunny reluctantly drew back. "I'll see you Monday." She gave him a quick peck on the lips before he could delay her further, then she bent down to pick up Oats' leash.

She and her dog made their way only a few steps to the sidewalk before Sam called out to her once more. "You mean I'll see you *tomorrow.*"

She stopped, and hope sparked in her heart. "Tomorrow?" she asked, cocking her head. "But I'm off tomorrow."

He grinned. "I know. You're off from work, but you're not off the hook from your swim lesson."

Her mouth dropped open, and Sam laughed out loud at her expression.

Swim lesson? Oh, no! She had forgotten all about Sam giving her swim lessons. Was it that time already? She was about to tell him that she wasn't sure tomorrow was such a good day, but he had already turned away and was walking back up the front porch steps.

Once he reached the front door, he turned around with a wicked grin that would have made her sigh if she wasn't having an attack of nerves and wasn't consumed with thoughts on how to gracefully chicken out of tomorrow's lesson.

As if reading her mind, he pointed a finger at her and, with a playful grin, added, "Don't be late."

Sunny stepped outside and held out the palm of her hand. "Uh-oh. Looks like rain."

Sam looked up at the sky, squinting at the blazing sunlight. "Oh, yeah, looks like a regular monsoon coming," he said dryly.

She gave him a guilty shrug. "Well, you know how it is with summer showers around here. The sun can be out one minute and then—*bam*—all of a sudden there's thunder and lightning."

He rolled his eyes at her obvious attempt to get out of her swim lesson and nudged her forward. "I think we'll take our chances."

She dug in her heels. "Are you sure?" she asked, hugging her towel to her like a child with a teddy bear. "I wouldn't mind one bit if you wanted to postpone things until the conditions are better."

Sam put his sunglasses on and shook his head with amusement. Sunny was a piece of work. She wasn't even *trying* to put up a brave front. "Conditions are perfect. Be-sides," he said, gesturing to his kids waiting on the dock, "you don't want to show Emma and Cole you're a chicken, do you?"

She bit her lip and looked to be debating this idea in her mind.

He laughed and swung his arm around her shoulders, guiding her up the path. "In case you didn't know, the cor-rect response to that is *no*," he whispered in her ear.

Sunny smelled so good—a combination of her coconut sunscreen and her lemony shampoo that had him sneaking an extra whiff before turning his head away. Sunny didn't share his chuckle, but he did feel her body relax a little under his arm.

"You're going to be fine," he said as soothingly as possi-ble. "I'm not going to let anything happen to you, okay?"

He *wouldn't* let anything happen to her. But that was an understatement. Sunny had become undeniably important to him. It was one of the reasons why he had given in to his attraction to her. Plus, she made his children happy. She made him happy. He hadn't experienced true happiness in a long time. He figured he deserved a little.

Even if it was only temporary.

Sunny nodded, though she looked so pitiful that a part of Sam did want to let her off the hook, but it was too impor-tant for her to learn. For her own safety and for the safety of his children, especially living so close to the water. He wasn't fooling himself. Today wasn't going to be easy, but he was determined. After all, he had taught both his kids how to swim, so he felt fairly confident in his ability with Sunny.

How different could it be?

As soon as Sunny removed her cover-up, he saw how different.

Sunny wore a two-piece bathing suit. Not quite a bikini, but nonetheless there was no place for him to put his hands on her that wasn't all skin. How could he concentrate and teach her to swim in that thing? Beads of sweat began to gather on the back of his neck as he entertained the thought of sending his children inside to watch a movie instead of the swim lesson.

Sunny looked over and caught him staring. "What?"

His eyes swept over her. "I think you know what."

She looked down at herself. She fluttered her eyelashes back up innocently, but her smile was coy. "Do you think it's too much?"

He snorted. "You *know* it's too little."

"Well, I just wanted you to know that I can be difficult too," she said with a grin.

Sam laughed. He loved that she was throwing his own words back in his face. For all her sweetness, Sunny could also be clever and funny. It seemed like he'd been laughing a lot since she started working for him. He'd even found it humorous when she threw his phone into the street—well, maybe not at the time, but now that he knew the reason why she did it. Sunny seemed to be truly concerned by the lack of attention he was showing his children. He hadn't been around a woman that selfless in a long time. Certainly not his ex-wife. Or even his own mother, for that matter.

But as much as he appreciated Sunny's loyalty to his kids and how concerned she was about their happiness, he wasn't going to foster any hope that theirs would be a real, lasting relationship. That was one of the reasons why he didn't want his children to see him showing Sunny any signs of affection. It wouldn't be fair to get their hopes up either. No matter how much he wanted to reach out and touch her right then.

Emma ran over to them grinning from ear to ear. "I like your bathing suit, Sunny. It's all sparkly and pink."

"Thanks, Emma," she said, shooting Sam a smug grin.

"Will you save it for me so I can wear it when I get older?" the girl asked.

Sam frowned. "No, she certainly will not!"

Sheesh! If he was ever looking for the proverbial ice water in the face, he found it right then and there.

That's all he needed to worry about. His daughter growing up to be as attractive to men as Sunny was to him. Fortunately, Emma was too young to understand his concerns—thank you, God—so when his daughter began to pout, he added more calmly, "Uh, styles change, sweetie. When you grow up, I'll get you an even prettier and, uh, more sparkly bathing suit."

Hopefully, by then, turtleneck bathing suits would be all the rage.

"Come on, you guys," Cole called from the dock. "Last one in smells like Emma's socks!"

Sunny's bathing suit forgotten, Emma laughed and took off running toward her brother.

Sunny turned to face Sam, suddenly squaring her shoulders and taking in a deep breath. "Okay. I'm ready," she told him, but her voice trembled.

He smiled. "Don't worry. We'll take your lesson slow today," he promised.

She nodded, looking up at him with her big blue eyes, wanting to trust him. He knew exactly how that felt— having that need to trust. It had been a long time since he'd trusted a woman. Women were never a safe bet for him, yet he couldn't help hoping this time would be different. He didn't really know whom he wanted to reassure more, Sunny or himself, but before he knew it, he gave in to an impulse and pulled her into his arms.

"Samuel!"

He and Sunny sprang apart just as quickly as they had come together. He blinked, not sure if he was more surprised by the fact that his mother was standing only three feet away or by the chastising tone she had just used on him.

Sam wanted to believe his mother was concerned about his children seeing him hug a strange woman in a bikini. Unfortunately, he knew better. His mom hated being left out of the loop as far as anything that went on in his life— personal or professional—and her sudden petulant attitude clearly expressed that point.

Sunny's cheeks flushed pink, and she tried to take a step back, but he hooked his arm around her waist, pinning her to his side. He and Sunny weren't doing anything to be ashamed of, and he'd be damned if he was going to let his mother make him feel as if they were.

Sam pasted on a smile. With her chin-length platinum hair and her lean, tennis-playing figure, Helen Calloway looked good for her age. She always had. But she had his money to thank for that. "Mom, what are you doing here? I thought you were going to be using my condo in New York."

Her lips thinned at his greeting. Based on her expression, his mother probably expected something a little more welcoming, but being taken off guard like this, neutral was the best he could do.

"Well, I was, but I changed my plans. I ran into your friend Mark, and he gave me some interesting information that I wanted to come and see for myself."

"Oh? And what information is that?"

She slowly changed her focus, her hazel eyes narrowing in on Sunny. "I believe I'm looking at it right now."

Chapter Ten

Sam's jaw tensed. Leave it to his mother to bring her flair for Broadway dramatics to the New Jersey countryside. However, Sunny didn't seem affected by his mother's cold attitude. She eagerly stepped forward, holding out her hand in a friendly gesture.

"I'm sorry, Mrs. Calloway, you must think I'm awfully rude," Sunny said with a tentative smile. "I'm Sunnyva Fletcher. Friends call me Sunny."

"Helen Calloway," his mother answered, taking Sunny's hand for only a second before pulling back.

"Sam hired me as the children's nanny for the summer."

His mother gave Sam a sly glance. "So I've heard, dear. But tell me, why, then, aren't you with the children *now*?"

Sunny jumped at her authoritative reprimand. "Oh. Yes, of course." She automatically turned toward the dock.

Sam jumped in front of her to keep her from walking away. "Today is Sunny's day off, Mom," he said, taking Sunny by the shoulder and spinning her back around. "She came here to spend the day with us so I could give her a swim lesson."

His mother raised her eyebrows a clear inch up her forehead but said nothing.

Sunny placed a hand on his arm to get his attention. "Um, look, why don't I go check on the kids and tell them their grandmom is here? Meanwhile, you can catch up with your mom, show her the house, and maybe get her something to eat or drink."

Sam hesitated. Sunny was right, but he didn't want their day to be interrupted like this. This was the first Saturday in a long time where he was completely taking the day off and nothing would be expected of him. Now, with his mother in town, it would only be a matter of minutes before some kind of request would be made of him.

He nodded anyway. "All right. It looks like your swim lesson will have to be postponed. Sorry about that."

Sunny gave him a brilliant smile, which made him ache that he wouldn't be spending more time with her today. "It's okay," she told him. "Believe me, I'm *not* sorry."

Sunny grabbed her cover-up and headed off down the path to the children. Once she was out of earshot, he tore his eyes away from her retreating back and faced his mother again.

She placed her hands on her hips and frowned at him. "You're surrounded by all this water, and your nanny doesn't know how to swim? Just what kind of agency would send a nanny like that out here?"

Sam sighed. "I didn't use an agency, Mom. I just sort of . . . found her."

"*What*? Found her? What's come over you? First you run off to the beach with little advance notice, and then you pull some woman off the street and put her in charge of taking care of *my* grandchildren? I can't believe you were duped like this. Haven't you learned anything from your experience with Kate?"

The outrage emanating from his mother's surgery-enhanced face was comical, although Sam didn't feel like laughing. At the mere mention of the turbulent time spent with his ex-wife, Sam's stomach muscles tensed into one giant knot. He didn't need to be reminded of Kate. Not now. And certainly not by his mother.

"Sunny is not some homeless woman, and she's not Kate," he said more harshly than was necessary. "What do you really know about first impressions? Your character judgment isn't exactly impeccable. As I recall, you were all too happy to introduce me to Kate back then. And look what it got me."

His mother flinched. Then after a long moment, her expression grew soft. She stepped closer and laid a hand on his arm. "I'll tell you what it got you—two wonderful children," she reminded him.

His shoulders sank. Then he took in a deep, defeated breath. "Yeah, I know," he whispered.

His wonderful kids. His mom was finally right about something. Emma and Cole were the only good to come out of a marriage that had been filled with resentment over inflated expectations. The *only* good thing that Kate was too blind to acknowledge. Sam might have forgiven Kate for not loving him enough to make their marriage work, if only she had shown an ounce of compassion for their children.

"Bunny is very pretty," his mom said, breaking into his sulking thoughts. "Mark told me she was and that you two might be involved. You've become infatuated with her."

"Her name's *Sunny,* not Bunny. And how did Mark become

such a know-it-all love guru? I never mentioned I was infatuated with her—or with anybody, for that matter."

"Mark didn't have to tell me that," she said, giving him a
shrewd grin. "I'm old, Sam, but not blind. Besides, I think I
can read my own son's body language. You're very protective of her. Just how long have you known her anyway?"

"Long enough." Although not really long at all. He'd
only known Sunny for about a month, so he couldn't explain
his protective reaction. Feelings came over him whenever
Sunny was involved. Feelings he didn't want to have to explain, either. He wasn't ready to reach inside himself to find
out what they were.

Done with his mother's probing questions, he decided to
cut to the chase. "Why are you really here, Mom? There
isn't a Lilly Pulitzer boutique around here for miles, so
don't tell me you're doing some window-shopping."

His mother glanced away and sighed. For a brief second
she looked pained and worn out, showing every wear and
tear of her sixty-two years, and also reminding him that she
was still his mother and he should treat her more kindly. No
matter how she acted toward him.

An apology for his scornful remark was on the tip of his
tongue, but she held up a hand to block it as if she sensed
it coming. "I only came here because I was worried about
you," she told him. "And because I wanted to see my grandchildren."

Sam folded his arms and waited. He was expecting the
standard *and because I need and/or want something* statement to follow, but to his surprise, no other words came out
of his mother's mouth.

Her gaze turned toward the water, and when she saw Sunny
leading Emma and Cole back to the house, she smiled warmly

at his children. "I left my bags in the car, Sam. I'm going to meet a friend in Atlantic City next weekend. If you have the room, I'd like to stay here with you and the kids until then." She hesitated a moment before adding, "If it's okay with you, that is."

Words failed him. If he wasn't staring at her in the flesh, he would have sworn on a stack of Bibles that this woman was not his mother. Well, what do you know about that? His mother actually wanted to spend some time with them.

"*Is* it okay?" she asked, looking unsure.

"Of course, Mom." He smiled, and this time it was genuine. "The kids and I would love to have you."

"Grandma!" His children's voices rang out behind them. They both came running up, and his mother knelt on one knee with her arms open wide.

Sunny had been slowly trailing behind them as if she wanted to give their reunion some privacy. Glancing at the children with his mother, Sunny sidled up to him with a smile. "It's nice that your mother came to visit," she whispered. "The children are very excited."

Sam just grunted in response. Yes, his children were excited to see his mother, but he was still waiting to see if it was *nice* that she came to visit. As much as he wanted to, he couldn't trust his mother's reason for coming.

Emma gave his mother another hug and then immediately started rambling. "Grandma, did you bring your bathing suit? Daddy is going to teach Sunny how to swim, but me and Cole already know how. Do you want to watch us? I don't even have to hold my nose anymore when I go under."

"Easy does it, kiddo," Sam said with a laugh. "You can show Grandma how you swim, but Sunny's swim lesson is canceled for today."

Cole and Emma both groaned in protest. "Oh, why?" Cole asked. "But we don't want her to drown again."

His mother shot Sam a questioning look as she stood. "Drown . . . *again?*"

Sunny's cheeks flushed pink. "Uh, I should really get going."

Cole frowned. "Aren't you going to stay?" he asked Sunny.

Sunny shook her head, ruffling his wet hair. "No, Cole. This is strictly a family day for you guys."

"But you *are* family," Emma protested. Then she turned to Sam with pleading eyes. "Tell her, Daddy. Tell her she's family and that she can stay."

In a way, it felt like Sunny was part of the family. His lips parted to tell her just that, but Sunny interrupted him.

"No," she told them gently. "Another time, guys. I promise." She glanced with some uncertainty at his mother. "It was nice meeting you, Mrs. Calloway—er, Helen."

"It was nice meeting you too," his mother replied stiffly.

Emma tugged on her grandmother's hand. "Come on, Grandma! You have to come watch us swim."

His mother laughed. "Oh, okay. Let's go."

Once Sam and Sunny were alone, Sunny turned to him with a frown. "You know, I don't think your mom likes me."

Sam shrugged. "She likes to intimidate. It's an old, skilled, country-club technique."

"No," she said, cocking her head to one side in thought. "I think there's more to it than just that."

"I wouldn't worry about it. My mother hardly ever does anything without an ulterior motive, but I doubt true concern for my feelings is her reason for snubbing you."

"Oh, Sam, what a terrible thing to say! Of course she's concerned for you. She's your mother."

An odd sense of guilt spread through him. Sam gazed out to the dock where his mother sat, smiling and clapping at his children showing off in the water. His heart softened a little toward her just then, but he quickly looked away to keep his feelings in check. He didn't want to form any expectations from his mother's visit this time. That would only lead to more disappointment, more pain. He didn't want to go there.

"Look, don't concern yourself over it," he told her. "My mother will grow bored here soon enough and be on her way back to the city." Just like he and the children would go back to the city. They'd all go back to their old life, and Sunny would too. Sunny would find another job. Maybe another nanny job. She'd probably even meet another man, and maybe—

He didn't want to go there either.

Sunny bit her lip, still looking unsure. His gaze automatically flew to her mouth, and then he was reminded of what he'd wanted to do since she'd first come over today.

He grabbed her hand and tugged her toward the house. "Come on," he said with a grin. "Let's not waste this time. I want to go inside so I can give you a proper good-bye without anyone seeing or interrupting us."

She grinned back. "Oh? What exactly is a proper good-bye?"

He slid open the back screen door and winked. "I'll just have to demonstrate."

"You have lip gloss on your neck."

Sam's hand sprang up, and he blindly tried to rub it off. "Thanks," he mumbled sheepishly.

How had his mother noticed lip gloss? She wasn't even

looking at him. She was just reclining on a lounge chair watching his kids swim. In fact, she had barely glanced his way since he'd returned outside after Sunny left.

His mother continued to keep her focus on the children. "The kids are getting so big, Sam," she said with a sigh, changing the subject. "I've decided that I want to be more of a presence in their lives. I could even watch the kids for you this year when they come home from school."

"I never said you couldn't be more of a presence in their lives. It's always been your choice."

She nodded. "Good. If I were around more, I think it would add some stability to Emma and Cole's environment. It might make things easier if I lived closer, but I'm not sure I can afford a condo near or in your building."

Sam's guard went up along with his annoyance. If his mother wanted him to buy her a condo, he wished she'd just come right out and ask like she normally would. But he reined in his ire and tried for a neutral response. "Stability is important."

"Yes. I think stability is important for them too." She finally sat up and turned, taking off her sunglasses to look him in the eye. "Sam, do the children know that you're seeing Sunny outside of work? You know, romantically?"

Sam huffed out a breath. They were back to this again. He didn't know what she was up to, but he didn't like it. "No, as a matter of fact, they do not know."

"Well, thank goodness for that. It's not good to have these women coming in and out of their lives, giving them false hope. They're looking for a mother."

"I know they are," he said with a sigh. Part of him felt guilty for not entertaining the idea of ever getting married again. They deserved a mother. He didn't doubt Sunny would make a good one someday, but just not to his kids. But he would make it up to them in his own way. Somehow.

"Are you in love with her?" his mother asked.

Sam flinched at the question. *In love with Sunny?* He stared at his mother, an answer hesitating on his tongue.

Why was he hesitating?

What he felt for Sunny was different than what he'd felt for Kate, but it couldn't be called love. How could it be love? He and Sunny hadn't even known each very long.

He was attracted to her, for sure, and loved various things about her, like how she cared for his children, her dedication, her loyalty, and her kindness. He wanted to be with her. That much he knew too. But he couldn't call it love. He *wouldn't* call it love.

No matter how much he wanted—just this one time—to acknowledge what was in his heart. He wasn't ready.

"I'm not in love with Sunny," he answered with more force than he'd intended. Then he shook his head to seal his point and rid the thought from his mind for good.

His mother's shoulders relaxed, and she sat back. "Well, good. Because you have to be careful. You're a very successful man with two small children to think about. Gold diggers like Kate are everywhere. Some of them even live in small towns and dress up like princesses."

He looked at her sharply. "How do you know about Sunny working as a princess?"

"Emma and Cole told me how you all met Sunny at the boardwalk. She couldn't have been making much money there. You offering her a nanny position was the equivalent of her hitting the lottery, and judging by the lip gloss on your neck, she probably wants much more than a mere paycheck."

Sam sat forward and rubbed his head. The accusations his mother was throwing at him were giving him a headache. If he'd had half a clue his Saturday was going to turn out like this, he would have gotten some work done in his office instead. Although he supposed he couldn't get too upset at his mother's line of thinking. After all, he had had similar suspicions when he first met Sunny.

"Sam, she wants something from you," his mother finished.

No! his mind screamed. It was something he couldn't accept, and it broke the dam of his anger. He dropped his hands and looked at his mom, resentment bubbling up to his throat. "Well, you would know best about that, wouldn't you?"

His mother's chin jutted out. "What's *that* supposed to mean?"

"Nothing," he muttered as he stood. "I think I've had enough sun for the day."

Cole climbed out of the water and walked up to him, dripping heavily the whole way over. "Where are you going, Daddy?"

He reached down and squeezed his son's shoulder. "I need to take care of a few things inside. Don't worry, Grandma will watch you." Sam gave his mother a sidelong glance. "It's the least she could do for me."

Seeing Kelly Green and her friend Tiffany walk into the Blowfish Tavern didn't dampen Sunny's good mood one bit. Sunny didn't care how unskilled they both thought she was. It didn't matter anymore. Sam seemed to like her just as she was—dishpan hands and all. In fact, if that good-bye kiss he'd given her this afternoon was any indication, she'd say Sam *more* than just liked her.

Kelly and Tiffany took a table in the back. But before Kelly sat down, her eyes narrowed at Sunny. Sunny smiled and waved to her, which turned Kelly's glare to full-on if-looks-could-kill mode.

Sunny chuckled to herself as she turned away. Maybe she was asking for trouble, but she couldn't help herself. Her spirits were high, and she felt untouchable.

She was in love. In love with Sam Calloway.

Imagine that . . . The more she thought about it, the more accustomed to it she became. And the more she liked the feeling. Now, if only Sam would admit the same thing to himself and to her, she'd like the feeling a whole lot more. Still . . . she couldn't help thinking her grandmother was smiling down at her at this very moment.

Suddenly, fingers snapped in front of her face.

"Yo, princess," said, Dave, the bartender, "you come here tonight to work or daydream?"

Sunny blinked and blushed. "Oh, sorry, Dave. I was just—"

"I know what you were doing," he said with a wry grin that showed his chipped front tooth. "But you could at least *try* to look like your mind isn't anywhere else but here."

Dave winked at her, then resumed filling up his bowl of sliced limes and lemons. He was a burly man of about six-foot-two with biceps bigger than Sunny's thighs. He worked as a fireman in town but moonlighted as a bartender whenever the owners needed extra help in the summer. Although he rarely joked with her, Sunny liked him. He always treated her kindly, especially when she made mistakes—which was often.

Sunny gave him a mock salute. "For you, Dave, I'll try."

He shook his head and smiled. "You're a good kid." Then he leaned both his elbows on the bar and tipped his chin toward the tables behind her. "So tell me. What did you do to get old Kelly Green's panties twisted up in a knot? Steal her boyfriend?"

She planted a hand on her hip. "Oh, come on. Do I look like the boyfriend-stealing type?"

"Nah, but *she* sure does. I'd watch my back with her, princess." His gaze traveled over her shoulder. "Hey, speak of the devil. Here comes your boyfriend now."

Sunny's heart leaped to her throat. Sam was here to see her! She quickly ran her hand through her bangs a few times, then spun around, ready to run into Sam's arms. But Flea stood in front of her instead. Her face fell.

Flea's mouth gave a wry twist. "Gee, don't look so excited to see me. I'll get a big head."

Despite her disappointment, she chuckled. "I'm sorry, Flea. I—I just thought—"

"That I was Sam?"

She shrugged guiltily.

Flea didn't look jealous at all. In fact, he seemed to have something else on his mind. "Listen, do you have a minute to talk?"

Sunny glanced back at Dave, who waved her away with his hands. "Go, go," he said. "I got ya covered."

Sunny followed Flea to a table on the other side of the bar. When she sat down, Flea sank back in his chair, his expression taking on a sudden seriousness she wasn't used to. "I've got some news," he announced.

"What kind of news?"

He suddenly couldn't meet her eyes. His head ducked slightly, and he began fiddling with the ends of the tablecloth. "I, uh, have been kind of seeing the assistant dean over at the College of Medicine and Science lately."

A mixture of surprise and relief filled her. No wonder Flea wasn't jealous of Sam. Flea had a girlfriend. She let out an audible sigh. *Thank goodness.* Kim must have been wrong about Flea having feelings for her. Just as Kim was wrong about Sam hurting her.

Sunny sat back with a grin. "That's your news?" she asked, folding her arms. "You had me worried there for a second."

His cheeks flushed. "Well, no. Well, sort of. We've, uh, been talking about you."

"Whatever for?"

He finally lifted his chin and looked at her with wary eyes. "She told me you sent in your application and transcripts and that the school was very impressed with them."

"Really?"

Flea nodded. "Sunny, I hope you don't mind, but I told her about your finance issues. She said that if you want to go there, they have a program where they'd pay for your education if you agree to work for the school after graduation for at least five years before going into private practice. Now, before you get mad at me, let me say that I think this is a great opportu—"

Sunny held up her hand. "Wait. They'd *pay me* to attend college?"

"Well . . . I guess you could say that. But it's not like—"

Sunny jumped out of her chair and planted a big kiss on Flea's surprised face. "Oh, thank you, Flea!"

"Take it easy, Sunny," he said, laughing. His already

ruddy face turned a shade darker. "I hoped you'd be happy and not upset at what I'd done. But you still have to actually take the courses and pass," he said, shaking a finger at her.

"Oh, I will! It's like a dream. I don't know what to say!"

He chuckled. "You don't have to say anything, Sunny. Your undying gratitude is thanks enough," he said with a twist of his mouth.

"Well, you definitely have that. And then some," she added with a wink.

Sunny's heart was so full, she thought it might burst at any second. Things were finally changing for her. Her life was getting in order. She could almost feel that bad-luck cloud shifting away from her. Her grandmother would be so proud to know that she was finally going back to school. And thanks to Flea, she could afford to go.

Her thoughts drifted to Sam and what he would say when he found out. She bet he'd be surprised, but he'd be just as proud too. A hotshot business mogul and a soon-to-be veterinarian didn't sound like such an unlikely match in her mind. Soon she'd be able to stand on her own two feet financially. Not only that, but she'd be doing what she loved. Becoming a veterinarian was her dream job.

Now if she could only get her dream *man*, her happily-ever-after would be complete.

Chapter Eleven

Sam had to get out of the house. He'd felt edgy and restless ever since the conversation he'd had with his mother about love this afternoon. He needed to think. He certainly couldn't do that with his mother around, throwing questions at him every two seconds. So, after he kissed his children good-night, he decided to go for a drive. He didn't know exactly where to go. Eight o'clock was early on a Saturday night. But when he stopped at a gas station, he immediately asked for directions to the Blowfish Tavern, and then there he was.

And there *she* was.

Sunny was leaning her elbow on the bar, listening to something the bartender was saying. Then she threw her head back and laughed. Just the sound of it made his heart leap, and he couldn't wait to rush over to her. Instead, he paused in the doorway. Sam was already concerned about his inexplicable need to draw comfort from her presence, and now the sound of her voice was weaving that spell further around him.

Why had he really come here anyway?

He shifted his footing as he rubbed a hand over his face. He had never felt more at a loss for what to do about his feelings. For so long he'd closed himself off to people—learned to rely on himself. But here he was, like an addict, hoping to talk to Sunny, surround himself in her tenderness, and gain some sort of relief. But relief from what?

Sam let out a quiet breath. His mother was right. He shouldn't have gotten romantically involved with Sunny. He thought he could have a temporary relationship with her. But for some reason the very thought of leaving Sunny after the summer made his chest hurt.

His mind was going haywire. He shouldn't have come here. He would have never come to any other woman's workplace. This was a sign. A sign that he needed to pull back before someone got hurt.

"Excuse me, but are you Sam Calloway?"

Sam blinked, then looked at a petite blonde smiling up at him with bright cherry lips. Her perfume bore the heavy scent of lilies and made his eyes begin to water. She seemed vaguely familiar. In fact, he might have seen her working in one of the stores downtown.

"Yes," he answered politely. "I'm sorry, have we met before?"

She smiled wider, her teeth glowing white against her red-stained lips. "Well, not officially. But you did drop off some shirts to be cleaned at my store." She formally held out her hand. "I'm Kelly Green. I own Shamrock Cleaners in town. It's not often we get a celebrity to come and stay in our little town," she drawled.

Sam gave her a weak smile. "I hardly think I'm a celebrity."

"Oh, but you are! I subscribe to *Forbes* magazine—seeing

that I'm a business entrepreneur too—and I see your name mentioned all the time. Of course . . . you're much better-looking in real life than in that magazine. You must be bored out of your skull down here when you could be back home in exciting New York City."

Sam's guard went up at her obvious admiration for his success. He never thought of New York as exciting. But then again, he wasn't one to take advantage of the nightlife the city offered. New York was just a convenient place to live because of his business. Although he supposed he didn't need to be in the office as much as he had been. Things seemed to be working out with him here in Ocean Bluff just as well as when he'd been living closer to the office. He might even be able to take off like this every summer and come here. He would hardly call this town boring. In fact, he was beginning to grow quite attached to it.

Thinking of attachments, Sam let his gaze travel over to Sunny again. She still hadn't noticed he was in the bar area. The bartender was showing her the best way to balance six beers on a tray, and Sunny seemed to be breaking into a sweat trying to copy him. Sam couldn't help but smile at her poor attempts.

Kelly followed the direction of Sam's gaze. "How is your nanny situation working out? I would hope Sunny's children-watching is far better than her beer-balancing. Has she had any more near drownings?"

Surprised, he swung his gaze to Kelly. "I wasn't aware that anybody knew what had happened."

"Well, sure, hon," she said with a shrug. "You can't run to the grocery store in this town without everybody knowing what you're having for dinner. Sunny was lucky to keep her fear of water hidden for such a long time. Too bad she wasn't so good keeping at her finances a secret. But I suppose if you don't pay your property taxes and almost lose your house because of it, word is going to spread fast."

Sam frowned. "She almost lost her house?"

"Ooops." Kelly raised her fingers to her mouth with wide eyes. "I thought that's why you hired her. Because you felt sorry for her. The word around town is that she's in debt up to her eyeballs. She would do just about anything for work these days, you know, because she needs the money so badly."

She would do just about anything . . .

Sam's heart slammed up against his ribs, the force of it almost affecting his balance. Sunny was in debt. Of course. No wonder she worked another job, even though he was paying her beyond what was considered average pay for a nanny. She needed the money.

His ex-wife, once a struggling model, had needed money too. She had used his connections for her career and then, once she'd become successful herself, had little time for Sam and the children.

He rubbed his temples, trying to remind himself that Sunny wasn't Kate. They were two totally different people. Sunny wasn't after his money. Somewhere deep inside he wanted to believe that, but old habits died hard, especially after what he'd been through with Kate and now his mother. He couldn't risk his heart and find out that he'd been wrong about Sunny. He had been made the fool one too many times in his life already.

Why hadn't Sunny mentioned her problem to him? That question nagged him the most. Was she waiting for the right time when he had grown closer to her? Would she have asked him for a raise then, or would she have just come right out and asked him for a loan? Maybe even ask for a condo like he knew his mother would? Whatever the answers were to those questions, he needed to hear them now.

Sam blindly turned away. "Excuse me," he murmured to Kelly.

Kelly called something to him, but it didn't register. His mind was swimming, and his feet felt as though he were wearing lead shoes as he made his way toward the bar.

Sunny flipped her hair off her shoulders, then, as if sensing him coming, glanced his way. Her face lit up, and she rushed over to him. "Sam! Oh, I'm so glad you're here. Flea stopped by a little while ago. I'm so excited. I have something to tell you."

"Yeah," he said grimly. "I have something to tell you too."

Sunny blinked. Then she hung back slightly, worrying her lip as she studied his face. "Is everything okay? Is your mom all right?"

Sam forced himself to look away from her sympathetic face. Sunny had a way of bringing his guard down. But he had already opened himself too much to her. Trusting her. He'd almost made the mistake of opening up even more before he ran into Kelly Green. He didn't know what to believe about Sunny's character, but he wouldn't allow himself to be sucked into any kind of false concern now. He needed answers first. Not only did he have his own heart to think about, but also the hearts of his children.

"My mother's fine," he murmured. "Can we go outside and talk?"

Sunny glanced over her shoulder to the bartender, who rolled his eyes and nodded to her unasked question. Even though she obviously had permission, she still hesitated before turning back to Sam. "Um, sure," she said.

She and Sam stepped outside together. The ocean winds

must have shifted, because the air temperature had dropped dramatically. Sunny rolled down her sleeves and hugged herself to ward off the chilly breeze. Something felt off, but it wasn't just the unusual weather pattern. Sam seemed distant. Acting even cooler than when she had first met him. She wondered if it had anything to do with the amount of tension surrounding him and his mother.

"I'm really glad you stopped by," she said, hoping to get him to smile. "I missed you." The strange, stoic resignation in his face didn't change, so she took a deep breath and braced herself for whatever Sam apparently had on his mind. "I've some great news to share, but it can wait if you need to talk."

He looked away, but not before she caught a flare of steeliness in his eyes. "Yes, well, I did come here to talk, but I'm afraid I don't have good news to share."

A crushing feeling began to form in her chest. *Oh, no!* Was something wrong with one of the children? "What is it, Sam? Tell me."

Sam kept his eyes on the ground and spoke through clenched teeth, as if every syllable hurt his jaw. "I'm going to be heading back to New York earlier than expected. I'm afraid the children and I won't need your services any longer."

She staggered back a step, feeling as though she'd been hit by a bullet. "What?"

Sam finally looked up. But when their gazes met, his stony expression softened. "I'm sorry, Sunny," he said with a sigh. "You did a good job for us, but something's come up. I've decided to take time off from work next week and then head back home."

"But I thought you couldn't do that. You were busy with work. The children—*you*—needed me."

"Well, I *thought* I needed you. But I don't know. My mom will be here for a while to help me out before I leave. Of course, if you need any references, I would be happy to supply them for you."

References? Sam wanted to talk references? How could he be so callous? So cold? He was breaking up with her and leaving town for good with his children. Tears began to gather in her eyes. She wanted to cry, but everything was happening so fast, she had to make sure what he was saying was real.

"But what about . . . *us*?" she croaked.

"I'm sorry about that too. This wasn't what I had planned, but it's probably best we cool things off a little earlier than expected, since we both knew it was only going to be temporary anyway."

She nodded, not trusting her voice. If Sam only knew the truth. Their relationship, her feelings for him, had become serious. To her. And she definitely didn't want temporary. She wanted forever. Even now, as he treated her like a employee.

"It's not like you really need the nanny job anyway," he added. "You have this tavern job at least to get you by."

She remained silent, not wanting to elaborate on the financial problems she had gotten herself into or how much she needed the nanny position until she found another job and started school. Sam didn't want to hear her problems now. He was too focused on pushing her away. And she didn't want any of his pity.

His mouth took on an unpleasant twist. "I'm sure a frugal person like yourself has probably saved up quite a nest egg with all the odd jobs you've been working."

The anger in his tone caught her attention. "What's this really all about, Sam?"

He folded his arms. His voice was low and flat. "When were you going to tell me about the debt you've gotten yourself into? When you finally got the courage to hit me up for a loan?"

Sunny suddenly felt sick and hurt. She understood what Sam's anger was all about just then. Sam thought she was using him—that she only wanted to be around him because he was rich and she had money problems. He had confided similar fears to her days ago when he'd told her how he wasn't used to people wanting to be around him without having a hidden motive or agenda. But she had hoped he would never have to question her motivations for wanting to be with him. She had hoped he would trust her feelings for him. Trust *her*.

Apparently that wasn't going to be the case. But because she understood the scars from his past, she couldn't get defensive or angry toward him.

Sunny reached out and stroked his rough cheek. "I would never do that to you, Sam. I care about you too much."

His eyes went wide, and his lips parted as if in shock. But nothing came from his lips—especially not an *I care about you too*.

"Isn't that enough?" she asked. "Do my finances really matter?"

He quickly turned away. "Yes. No. I don't know." He placed his face in his hands for a moment and sighed. "Maybe as your employer it wasn't any of my business. But all this time we were growing closer, and you never confided in me. Never trusted me. What else am I supposed to think?"

"You could think I was at least trying to keep an ounce of my pride."

"Is that the real reason you didn't want to go to the hospital after you almost drowned? Because you couldn't afford to go?"

Her cheeks burned, and her voice shrank to barely a whisper. "Yes, that was the reason."

He nodded, but his eyes shimmered with disappointment and pain. "You should have told me the truth. Not that any of that matters now. It's best we end things—professionally *and* personally—before we have any more misgivings."

"Oh, Sam!" she cried. "I just didn't want to burden you with my problems. I wasn't trying to deceive you. I don't know what else to say or how to convince you I'm telling the truth. Don't push me away. Not over something like this."

But he had already begun to walk away, so she knew that any further explanation would be futile. She closed her eyes and sighed. She couldn't bear to watch another person she loved leave her life. Her heart seemed to crack, and a fresh attack of pain she hadn't felt since her grandmother died coursed through her. But she had to pull herself together and quickly go back to work. She couldn't afford to lose this job too.

Turning on her heel, she made her way back to the tavern entrance. She kept her focus straight ahead, her breathing even, and tried to compose herself before going back inside. Only when she reached the front door of the bar did she dare to look back over her shoulder into the parking lot. Sam's car was already gone.

"But I don't understand why Sunny didn't say good-bye to us."

Sam glanced down at Emma with a frown. It had been a little less than a week since he'd told the children that Sunny was finished being their nanny for the summer. But that didn't stop them from peppering him with questions about her nonetheless.

Maybe he'd been selfish in firing Sunny without letting her say good-bye to the kids. Heck, there wasn't any *maybe* about it. He *was* selfish. But he was hurt and had gone with his gut reaction, without thinking of the consequences or the pain his sudden decision would cause them.

Clearing the golf-ball-sized lump in his throat, he gazed at his daughter. "You never said good-bye to nanny Natasha," he reminded her.

"Yeah, but I don't *wuv* nanny Natasha."

A rush of emotion so intense coursed though Sam that it made him drop to his knees. How easy it was for children to declare their feelings. It wasn't so easy for him. When Sunny had told him she cared about him, he only gave her silence. But he had felt so used; everything he had experienced with his ex-wife came flooding to the forefront of his mind, and he panicked, firing her.

Sam truly envied his daughter's innocent heart, freely offering up her feelings on a silver platter for anyone willing to accept them, but at the same time he also wanted to protect her from the pain of heartache he knew too well. "Sweetie, you might think you love—"

"No!" To his surprise, Emma stamped her foot. "I *wuv* Sunny, and she *wuvs* us. I wanted us to all get married. Maybe if you say pretty please with hot fudge on top, she'll come back, and we can be a family."

Guilt and sadness over the attachment his daughter had for Sunny made his tongue grow dry and thick. He wanted to protect his kids, but it seemed he was too late. "No. I don't think that will do it. I know you and Cole liked Sunny, but she won't be coming back. I'm sorry."

Emma's chin dropped as she turned and walked toward the playroom. Sam knew exactly what his daughter was feeling: disappointment, hurt, frustration. He thought his system had already been through the wringer, but as he'd said the words "She won't be coming back," his insides cracked even further.

"Good heavens!" his mother exclaimed as she bounced into the kitchen, looking like she'd just come back from the hair salon. "You look positively green, Sam. Are you feeling okay?"

He wearily rubbed his eyes. "Yeah, I'm fine. Just a little headache."

"That's good. I would feel terrible about leaving you for the weekend if you were sick."

"You're leaving for the weekend?" he asked, noticing for the first time the carry-on bag slung over his mother's shoulder.

She reached out and patted him on the cheek. "You *aren't* feeling well, are you? Remember, I'm meeting my friend Lois in Atlantic City. It's her birthday, and we thought we'd take in a show and try our luck at the casinos."

"Oh, right," he said with a smile, trying his best to shake off the strange, sad funk he'd been in ever since he'd fired Sunny. "It must have slipped my mind."

His mother put down her bag and looked at him through shrewd eyes. "Sam, I know you. Nothing ever slips your mind. What's going on with you? Is it your nanny? The children told me she just up and left."

"Yeah, well, not exactly. I kind of *made* her up and leave."

His mother arched a perfectly penciled eyebrow at him. "Really? Well, I think that was a smart move on your part. I heard she has money trouble, so it's best you distance yourself from her to be safe. No matter how well-liked she is in town or how she got herself into debt."

He held up a hand. "Wait a minute," he said, narrowing his eyes. "How do you know about Sunny's financial situation? And, more important, what do you mean by no matter *how* she got herself into debt?"

"Oh, come now, Sam. This is a small town. If you want information, all you have to do is ask around. Which is exactly what I did, since you hadn't bothered to do it yourself. She's not a spender like Kate was. I'll give her that, at least. It seems as though your Sunny had a sickly grandmother with no health insurance. The situation is actually very sad, when you think about it."

Sam suddenly went limp and sank into the chair nearest to him. "Sickly grandmother?" he echoed softly.

"Uh-huh." His mother checked her watch and huffed out an impatient breath. "I have to go. Where are the kids? I want to kiss them good-bye."

Sam motioned to the playroom with his chin, too stunned over the news about Sunny to form any words. It had never occurred to him to find out why or how Sunny had gotten into financial trouble. Hearing the circumstances of it only added to the guilt he was already having over firing her.

A part of him told him to forget it. Forget what he was feeling. Forget *her.* It didn't matter how she'd acquired her money issues, because it still meant she'd want him to do something about them. People always looked to him for those kinds of answers.

But then another part of him . . .

Another louder part of him told him he was stubborn jerk and deserved every single minute of the awful war raging inside him.

His mother startled him by laying a hand on his forehead. His mind swirling with thoughts of Sunny, he hadn't heard her come back into the kitchen.

"You look about as well as Emma does," his mother said, tilting her head to get a better look at his face. "She looks as pale as you. Is she feeling all right?"

"Emma just misses Sunny, Mom. She'll be fine. We'll *all* be fine," he added louder, not sure whom he was trying to convince more.

His mother gave him a sympathetic nod and, with a stroke on his head, gently added, "I hope so, dear."

Chapter Twelve

Sam sat on the edge of Emma's bed and felt her head; she was burning up. Sam had to get to a store to get some more fever medicine. But his mother had left for Atlantic City hours ago, and Emma was in no condition to be moved. He needed help.

Emma stirred and moaned, and her eyelids fluttered open. "I want Sunny," she said hoarsely.

Sam heaved a sigh. A part of him wanted Sunny too— for more reasons than just help with the children now. He could admit that much. It wasn't like he could shut off his feelings for her like he was flipping a switch. But he couldn't stand around and wait to be lied to and used again. He had convinced himself he had done the right thing by getting her out of his life as soon as possible. The only problem he hadn't thought about was how it would affect his children. They obviously loved and missed her. And now Emma needed her. As much as he didn't want to do it, he had to call Sunny and see if she would come and be with his daughter now. But after the way he'd fired her at the Blowfish Tavern, he doubted she would even answer the phone if she knew it was him.

Sam leaned forward, pressing a gentle kiss to Emma's hot cheek. "I'll be right back," he whispered.

When he walked out of the room, Cole was standing there, waiting for him, his arms filled with boxes of Legos. "I'm going to make Emma a pirate ship," he announced.

Sam smiled at his son's eagerness to cheer his sister up. "Why a pirate ship?"

"Because pirate ships are cool! And if I was sick, it would make me feel better if someone made *me* one."

"Does Emma like pirate ships?" he asked his son incredulously.

Cole's face fell, and his gaze lowered to the floor. "No. She likes girly princess stuff."

"Well, how about you make her something she *would* enjoy, then?"

"I guess so," he said with a frown. Then, after a few seconds, his face brightened again. "Hey, maybe I can make a princess castle *with* a pirate ship."

Sam chuckled, ruffling his son's hair. "That sounds like a great idea."

As Cole happily went into his room, Sam pulled out his phone and dialed Sunny's number. He held his breath as it rang, wondering how she would react. Would she do this favor for him after the way he had fired her? Or would she just hang up on him? He wouldn't really blame her if she did the latter.

Sunny picked up on the second ring. "Hello?"

He honestly didn't know what to say or how to begin. The friendly, musical quality of her voice caught him off guard. She sounded like a woman without a care in the world. But, then again, for as long as he'd known her, she had never let on that she was in debt, overworked, or even in danger of losing her home.

"*Hello?*" she repeated.

"Sunny." He cleared his throat as his grip tightened on the phone. "It's me, Sam."

Obviously he wasn't very good at hiding the stress of the situation in his voice, because she immediately blurted, "Oh, my gosh, Sam! What's wrong? What's happened?"

"It's Emma. She's sick. She's asking for you, and I—"

"I'll be right over." She quickly hung up the phone without any further information required.

"Thank you," he whispered into the dial tone.

Sam closed his eyes, a mixture of relief and shame filling his chest. The woman was a saint, a complete saint to do this. He didn't deserve the friendship she still gave to him, yet she gave it to him anyway, no questions asked. Why? Why would she do this? Her actions were foreign to him and messed with what he was so determined to believe about her.

For all his successful business dealings, Sam seemed to fail when dealing with his personal life.

Sunny gave Emma her last dose of medicine for the night, then pulled the blanket up to her shoulders. Her fever had broken a few hours ago after a lukewarm bath, but Sunny wanted to make sure it didn't come back in the middle of the night. Emma had even managed to eat a little soup, so Sunny figured the worst was over and the girl was on the mend.

After she tucked Emma in and said good night, Sunny checked on Cole and then made her way downstairs to the kitchen. Sam was cleaning up from dinner.

Sunny had come to Sam's house with a bag of ingredients to make her grandmother's Scandinavian turkey soup and got right to work on it as Sam drove to the pharmacy to get acetaminophen and ginger ale for Emma. All afternoon, they had taken turns checking in on Emma and entertaining Cole, but even with all her help, Sam still looked drained and exhausted.

Sunny quickly grabbed a dish towel off the kitchen island and began drying a stockpot. "I think Emma will be fine by tomorrow," she said to Sam's back. "It was probably just one of those twenty-four-hour things."

Sam nodded, his focus on rinsing the last of the bowls. Without a word, he handed it to her and dried his hands. He walked over the refrigerator and took out an open bottle of wine. Once he set it on the counter, he finally looked up at her. His face was pale, and the fine lines around his eyes seemed more pronounced than usual.

"Join me?" he asked, gesturing to the wine.

She bit her lip, hesitating for just a moment. She wasn't really a drinker, but the pleading look on his face did her in. "Well, maybe just a tiny bit."

Sam set two large goblets down and, ignoring her request, proceeded to fill them both up to the rim. When he finished, he slid her glass over to her with an amused grin. "I figured you could use this about as much as I can."

She eyed her wineglass skeptically. "Uh, thanks, but I don't think it was that bad. I'm sure Emma and Cole have been sick before."

"No, it wasn't that bad. But it could have been worse if you hadn't come. I usually have help in New York. I assure you, I will *never* take that help for granted again."

She smiled as Sam took a large mouthful of wine and swallowed. "I'm just glad it wasn't anything too serious. And I'm really glad you called me," she told him truthfully.

Sam's calling her when he needed help spoke volumes. Even though he had a hard time acknowledging it verbally, he trusted her with his children. She looked at that as an important step toward rebuilding their friendship.

Sam put down his wine and stepped closer to her, willing her to look him in the eyes. "I really appreciate what you did for Emma—well, for *all* of us. I'm sure you had other things you were supposed to do tonight. Maybe even—"

All of a sudden Sam's mouth went slack, and he slapped his forehead with a grunt. "Oh, no," he moaned. "You missed work, didn't you? Dammit, I'm sorry, Sunny. It didn't even cross my mind when I called you."

She quickly placed her hand on his arm. "It's okay. I was about due to have a sick day myself."

"Look, this is hard for me to say, but—"

"You're welcome," she said with a shy grin.

"I wasn't going to thank you."

She blinked. "You weren't?"

"No," he said with a chuckle. "Actually, I was going to say I'm sorry. I'm sorry for the things I said that night at the tavern. I'm sorry I fired you. Perhaps we both could have trusted each other more. I'd like to put it behind us. I only have a few weeks left here before I need to go back home. Maybe you could forgive me and come back to work here until then— like it was before."

Sunny wanted to sigh, but she sucked it back in. Sam was offering her back a desperately needed job but nothing else. It wasn't what she wanted to hear from him, but she rallied a smile anyway. "Sure. I'd like that."

"Good."

As they continued to smile into each other's eyes, Sunny felt a wistfulness building up inside her. She wanted to touch him then, wanted to convince Sam they still had a chance at a real relationship. They had more than chemistry. They were good together, taking care of the children like they had today—working as a team—like a real married couple. She only prayed Sam would realize it before it was too late.

Sunny reached for her purse, suddenly feeling the need for a little separation from Sam. Her daydreams were getting her carried away. It was probably best she leave while she still had her emotions in check. "Well, I should—"

"Stay," he said.

She slung her purse strap over her shoulder and froze. Her gaze darted to Sam's face, but he wouldn't look at her. He was frowning at his wineglass and seemed to be wrestling with his thoughts. Her own thoughts clattered in her brain, and her pulse quickened, but she didn't want to read anything more into his request for her to stay. Right now, he was just a worried father.

She cleared her throat. "I think the worst part is over. But I can drive over here first thing in the morning, if you like."

"No." He finally lifted his head and met her gaze head-on. So many emotions flickered in his eyes—emotions she wasn't used to seeing in Sam—that her breath caught.

"I want you to stay with me tonight," he said huskily. "Please."

The earnest look in his eyes alarmed her. There was no misreading his intent now. He sounded so desperate. He needed her, and her heart went out to him. But as much as she wanted to be with him, she had her heart to protect. Sam was still just offering her a night. Nothing more. This time she wasn't going to settle for temporary. She wasn't going to settle for coming in second in his life. Not this time around.

Her tongue suddenly felt dry and thick, and for a second she was worried if she would be able to tell him no. "I—I want to, but I can't," she managed.

She didn't wait for his response. Heartsick, she whirled around and started walking toward the door before he could talk her out of her decision.

"Sunny, wait!" he called. She stopped, hovering in the doorway. "I thought you said we could go back to how things were between us," he said.

She shook her head sadly. "No, Sam. I agreed I would go back to being a nanny for the children. I can't go back to the way things were between us. Not now."

"Why not? I missed you. The kids missed you. I thought you said you've forgiven me. I know I overreacted, but I'm asking you for a second chance."

"I *do* forgive you. And I more than missed you too. I love you." Her fingers flew to her lips. She hadn't meant to tell him like this—not when she was trying to walk out of his life.

"You love me?" At first his face paled, but then his lips tuned up into a triumphant smile. He stepped forward and took her in his arms.

"Well, I can't think of a better reason for a second chance for us," he said, kissing her tenderly on the forehead. "Don't you see? I want to be with you too. We can make this work for the little time we have left together. I told you before that I'm in."

She went very still, realizing that Sam still didn't trust her with his heart. She backed out of his arms, feeling sick and already missing the warmth of his body. "No. We can't make this work. Not this time. You see, whenever I say I care about you or love you, you say 'I'm in.' *That's* the problem, Sam. Normal couples do not build happily-ever-afters on those words."

Sam drew himself up straight, and his expression grew blank. He barely moved, but she could already see the barriers being set. He was resurrecting the wall around himself—that same wall she'd seen when she'd first met him. She knew what he was going to say before it even came out of his mouth.

"You've been playing prince and princess too much with the kids," he said sadly. "I'm not the man who can give you that fairy-tale happily-ever-after you want. The clock will strike midnight in two weeks when I have go back to New York, and then I, the kids, and this house will turn back into pumpkins. So why can't we just enjoy the time we have left? That's all I can give you."

For a long moment silence fell between them. She loved Sam so much that it hurt, and the pain inside her made it hard to breathe. It would be so easy to give him two weeks. Too easy to throw caution to the wind and enjoy that short amount of time together. But at the end of those two weeks, she couldn't go through losing Sam all over again. She realized now she deserved more than that.

"No, I don't want that, Sam," she finally said. "You don't give yourself enough credit. That's not all you can give me. That's all you *think* you can give me." Then, with all the courage she could muster, she turned around and walked out the door.

Only this time, Sam didn't try to stop her.

Kim froze in the middle of pouring herself a cup of coffee. "*What* did he say?"

Tears filled Sunny's swollen eyes all over again. She knew it was a bad idea to come to the coffee shop. But at least there wasn't anyone else sitting around them. The Sunday-morning crowd had already come in for their coffee-and-donut fill. The store was fairly quiet now.

Sunny hadn't planned to talk about her breakup with Sam in public, but she needed to see a friendly face. The solitude of her house only reminded her that Sam and the kids wouldn't be in her life anymore. Even the company of Oats wasn't enough for her.

"He said he was in," Sunny murmured, trying to control her trembling lips.

Kim took a sip of coffee and squinted. "*In?* In what? Did you forget to clean up after Oats?"

Sunny managed a small smile. "No, nothing like that." She swiped at her eyes, then leaned an elbow on the table, resting her chin in her palm. "Although that's what I thought at first too. To Sam, I think it was a declaration of affection."

Kim snorted. "Since when did 'I love you'—or even 'I *care* about you'—go out of style?" She slid a plate with a chocolate chip muffin under Sunny's nose, but Sunny shook it off.

Her insides were tangled up so tightly, she feared she wouldn't be able to eat for the rest of the day. Maybe the rest of the week. "He said it was the best he could do."

"Well, I hope you told him he could stick his best thing right up—"

"*Kim, please.*" Tears began to well up in her eyes again, only this time she couldn't hold them back any longer. "I need to be comforted. You're not comforting me. You're making me more upset."

"Oh, right!" Kim grabbed a wad of napkins and thrust them at her. "I'm so sorry, sweetie!"

Sunny took one of the napkins and dabbed her eyes. As she blew her nose, she was reminded of when she'd first met Sam's kids on the boardwalk and how Emma had blown her nose in her princess glove. More tears spilled down Sunny's cheeks. Even though she'd just seen the children last night, she missed them already. She never even had a chance to tell them good-bye.

Kim clucked her tongue. "I had a feeling he was bad news. A rich, workaholic father still pining after his dead wife does not make for a prime love-connection candidate, in my opinion."

Sunny sniffed into her napkin. "I don't know if Sam truly was in love with his wife."

"Lovely. So he's pining for a woman he didn't even love?"

"No, he's not pining for anyone." Which was why she was here crying in public to begin with. She loved Sam, and he . . .

"Sam loves me, but he's afraid to take a chance on that love," she finished out loud. "I know that's why he pushed me away. He's been hurt so many times in the past. I don't know what to do."

"Honey, there's nothing you can do. Sam has to make the decision to trust and love on his own. Although I think, with his track record, you shouldn't hold on to hope."

"But you were wrong about Flea having feelings for me, so maybe you're wrong about Sam too. Anything is possible, right? It's like that song."

" 'Disturbia'?"

Sunny smiled. "No, silly. 'Love Changes Everything.' "

"Then why is Sam moving back to New York, and you're sitting here crying in my coffee shop?"

Sunny looked away and sighed. "I don't know. I guess my love wasn't enough."

Chapter Thirteen

Sam had just finished cleaning up the breakfast dishes when his mother waltzed into the kitchen looking showered and freshly made up.

"What's all this?" she asked, gesturing to the row of suitcases lined up on the dining room floor.

"Exactly what it looks like," Sam said, pouring himself and her a cup of coffee. "The children and I are heading back to New York in a few days, so I thought I might as well get a head start on packing."

She checked her watch with a frown. "At seven-oh-five in the morning? My, but you are efficient."

"Efficient . . . and I couldn't sleep." He tiredly ran a hand over his unshaven face. "I've been up for quite a while."

"Yes, I know," she remarked, her eyes narrowing in speculation. "How's Emma feeling?"

"Apparently as good as new. She just downed an entire plate of scrambled eggs and bacon." Sam was still so thankful for Sunny's rushing to his aid. He didn't know how he would have managed two nights ago without her. He owed her so much.

But I sure had a funny way of showing her that, he reminded himself with disgust.

His mother nodded. "And how are *you* feeling?"

He glanced at her with surprise. "I'm fine," he told her. "I'm always fine." Never great. Never awesome. Just always . . . fine. Almost numb. Like his body was being perpetually shot with Novocain. He had forgotten that was normalcy for him. When Sunny was in his life, he had begun to feel a lot of emotions he'd thought his body had become immune to—and he had liked feeling each and every one of them again. But now it was back to business as usual.

His mother took a sip of her coffee and gave him a long look. "Samuel, why don't you tell me what's wrong."

"Nothing's wrong. I told you, everything's fine. In fact . . ." He picked up the packet of paperwork waiting for his signature and thrust it toward his mother. "I have something here that will completely brighten your day."

"What's this?" she asked.

"A condo lease. The best my money can buy."

His mother kept her hands at her sides and continued to frown at the papers in his hands. "You bought me a condo?"

"That's how it works, isn't it? You ask, and I supply. Well, enjoy."

"What on earth am I going to do with two homes? I don't remember ever asking you to buy me a condo."

"Well, maybe you didn't come right out and ask. But it was only a matter of time. I just saved you the trouble and time."

Anger flashed in her eyes, and she shoved the papers back at him. "I don't want the damn condo, Sam."

Sam tossed the papers on the counter and heaved a frustrated sigh. "Well, what do you want, then?"

"I'll tell you exactly what I want. I want my son in my life. I want *you*. Gosh, Samuel, that's all I ever wanted."

"Me?"

His mother walked over and lovingly stroked his cheek. "Yes, of course. Ever since you've become this corporate hotshot, I feel like we've drifted apart. You've treated me more like a business associate than a mother. The only time you give me your attention is when I need something from you. So maybe I appeared needier than I really was. But all I wanted was to keep some kind of connection with you." She smiled wryly. "You've always been very generous to me with your money. Not so generous with your *time*, though."

"That's not true," he said, stepping away from her reach. "I've always had time for you. You're my mother, for goodness' sake."

She sadly shook her head. "No, you didn't even want my help with the children after your divorce. You immediately went and hired a nanny."

Sam frowned, reeling from the revelation. Had he really pushed his own mother away? Maybe he had inadvertently. Not once had he considered asking his mother for help with the children. But being around her then had only made his resentment toward Kate more pronounced. He couldn't concentrate on work. It had been easier to just close off his feelings by avoidance and create a nice, thick box around himself. That method had worked well for him—up until he'd met Sunny. Sunny had managed to break down those defensive barriers. Now he was left exposed, and for once in his life, he didn't know how to face his emotions.

"After your father passed away, I didn't know what to do with my life. You were always working, so I joined some organizations to keep myself busy, but I was still so lonely for family. Because I was lonely, I thought you were lonely too, and that maybe you needed a wife—a family—to care for. When I met Kate waitressing at the country club, I thought she was such a nice girl and would be good for you. Obviously I rushed things and was mistaken. She had her own ambitions. But I honestly didn't know that about her. You have to believe I always had your best interests in mind."

"Yeah, I do know. I guess I never really doubted that. It was just easier for me to justify locking up my emotions if I didn't have anybody around me to call me on it. If I pushed you away, I'm really sorry, Mom. I haven't been fair to myself, to the children, to you—"

"To Sunny?"

He tensed at the mere mention of her name. "I don't know what you're talking about."

"Oh, come now, Samuel. I'm not going to have this lovely heart-to-heart with you and then have you suddenly clam up on me. You've been walking around like a zombie from *Night of the Living Dead*, and every time one of your children so much as mentions Sunny's name, you look about to break apart into tiny little pieces. I want you to finally be honest with me. Are you in love with her?"

"Yes."

There was no hesitation this time.

And it felt surprisingly . . . *good*. His breathing suddenly became easier—like the two-ton semi that had been parked on his chest had been lifted off.

"God help me, but yes," he said, enjoying how he felt the more he said the words aloud. "I am madly and deeply in love with that woman. I love how she hums the *Bob the Builder* theme song when she makes the children's lunch, I love how good she looks in a pair of yoga pants and flip-flops, I love how her smile can make me forget my worst day, and most of all, I love how she makes me feel whenever I'm around her."

His mother gasped, splaying a hand over her heart. Tears began to fill her eyes. "Oh, my dear son, I've never heard you express so much to me about a woman before. What are you going to do?"

"I think I've done enough," he said wryly. "I pretty much stomped on her feelings like a used cigarette butt. She told me she loved me, Mom, and I just pushed her away. I offered her her job back, but that was it."

"But she didn't take it back, did she?"

Sam didn't bother answering. He knew a rhetorical question when he heard one. Sunny didn't take her job back—even though he was sure she needed it. Which just went to show how much he'd hurt her. Sunny would rather starve than be in his presence for one minute longer than necessary.

"Sam, I have to be honest. I was skeptical about Sunny from day one. I think Kate did that to both of us. But I've reconsidered. After all, it's obvious she cares for my grandchildren. I don't think Kate—or even your average woman—would have responded to Emma's illness as quickly as Sunny did."

Sam hung his head and nodded. That was another thing he loved about Sunny: how she cared for his children. Emma and Cole were about as precious to her as they were to him. Then Sam gazed up into his mother's sympathetic eyes and realized something else: his mother loved him. Sam saw it right then and there and couldn't believe he had ever doubted it. He had pushed away his mother and had been wrong. And now he knew he had done the same thing to Sunny. Damn, he had been such a fool! Sunny loved him for exactly who he was, yet at the time he just couldn't accept it.

Sam was determined to go back to New York a different man now. He would work on repairing his relationship with his mother and devote more time to his children. Funny, but even with his new lease on life, he still felt a fine line of bleakness surrounding him. He should tell that to Sunny, and work on repairing their relationship too. But he knew it wouldn't make a difference to her. Not now. Would she even want to take a second chance on him after everything he'd put her through? She deserved so much better than that. Better than *him*.

"Well, have you made a decision as to what you're going to do?" his mother asked gently.

"Yes, I have," he said, walking over to the sink and dumping out the remainder of his coffee. "I'm going to go finish packing."

Sunny kept herself unusually busy the last few weeks of summer. Even though she was getting ready for her classes to begin, and her hours at the tavern had picked up, she still found the need to fill up more of her time. The more she worked, the less her mind would wonder off to Sam and the children, and the less chance she'd burst into tears—even if that meant filling her time by cleaning out her grandmother's garage.

The garage hadn't been organized in years. Considering she'd been working on it all Saturday afternoon, she hadn't made any real progress. But at least she'd sorted all the items into two piles. One pile of things that needed to be gone through—including boxes of her schoolwork and old trophies her grandmom had saved—and another pile of stuff that could be immediately thrown out.

Grabbing a broom to clear out some more cobwebs, she saw Oats shoot off the front porch and start barking. Sunny hoped Oats hadn't seen a rabbit. If that happened, her dog could be down the block already. She quickly dropped the broom and walked out to see what Oats was so fired up about. Oats continued to bark, and a few seconds later, Sunny froze when a black Volvo pulled up her driveway.

Sam.

Her heart pounded frantically, and she suddenly became self-conscious of her appearance.

But what was he doing here?

She wiped her dusty hands on her shorts and ripped the plaid kerchief from her hair, trying for a somewhat more civilized and less just-fallen-down-a-chimney-chute look.

Sam put the car in park, and Cole and Emma immediately jumped out. "Sunny!" Emma called brightly, running up to her.

"We came back from New York!" Cole shouted. "We missed you so much! Are you surprised to see us?" he asked, jumping up and down.

Surprised would be a mild word. Heart in her throat, Sunny could only smile and nod. Sam stepped out of his car then, and her world tilted further. He looked good— polished—dressed in khakis and a royal blue long-sleeved button-down. Her throat tightened further as she realized how much living in the city agreed with him. He took off his sunglasses, still hesitating by the car door. Their eyes met briefly, but she was sure she saw a strange combination of sadness and hope.

Emma caught Sunny's attention when the girl grabbed her by the waist and hugged her. "I missed you so much. We didn't have anybody to play princess with."

Despite the whirlwind of emotions coursing through her from their unexpected arrival, Sunny laughed. "I missed playing princess with you too."

"That's good," Emma said. "You don't have to worry, because Daddy brought your slippers with us, so we can all play forever."

"Play *forever*?" Sunny swallowed hard.

Cole bobbed his head up and down happily, not realizing the significance of what they were telling her. "Yeah, that's what Daddy said. He told us we came back so he could—"

"Cole, that's enough." Sam was suddenly next to them, tension radiating from his stance and his tone. In his hands—as his children promised—were the princess shoes Sunny had given his daughter when they had first met on the boardwalk.

Sam bent down and picked up one of Oats' old tennis balls in the grass. "Here," he said, handing it to Emma. "Why don't you and Cole go play ball with Oats while I talk to Sunny?"

Cole swiped the ball from Emma's hand and threw it across the yard. "Go fetch, girl!" Oats took off after the ball, and his children laughed as they ran off after her dog.

Sam turned his gaze back to Sunny, piercing her with his clear gray eyes. "As you can tell, the children missed you," he said with a wry grin.

"I know," she managed, her voice shaky. "I missed them too." *And I missed you.*

An awkward silence fell between them. It had been a few weeks since she'd seen Sam last, but just gazing at the man standing a mere two feet away took her breath from her. Even though there were tired markings around his eyes, Sam still looked so handsome with his face unshaven and his hair slightly windblown.

Sam tore his gaze away from hers, and with a smile glanced at her baggy T-shirt and jean shorts. "You look nice."

He sounded so sincere, she had to laugh. She didn't need a mirror to know she looked like Cinderella—pre-fairy-godmother days.

"Sam, what are you doing here?" she asked. "I thought you went back to New York."

"Well, I did. Or rather . . . I tried." He cleared his throat and took a step closer. "It didn't exactly work out, because I realized something."

"What did you realize?" she asked.

"I realized that I need you. So I'm here to offer you your old job back."

Sunny's heart constricted in her chest. *Oh, no.* She had gotten her hopes up *again.* Sam didn't really want to be with her after all. He just needed a nanny for his children.

Blinking back the tears in her eyes, she shook her head. "No, thanks, Sam. I think we've already been through this. I told you I'm not interested in a full-time nanny position, here or in New York."

Sam bit his lip and surprised her by looking rather shy. "Yes, I know that. That's why I'm not offering you the nanny position back. I told you I'm offering you your old job back instead."

She stared at him, trying to make sense out of what he was saying. "My old job back? You mean my Princess Miranda job?"

"Sort of. But I was thinking more along the lines of *Princess Sunny.*" Sam then held out the princess shoes to her.

When she made no move to take the slippers from his hands, he gently took her hand and wrapped her fingers around the straps. "Go ahead. Take the princess shoes," he told her.

Sunny did as she was told and then let her arms drop to her sides. She looked down at the shoes dangling from her fingers. The slippers were only made of plastic and ribbons, but at that moment it felt as if she had ten-pound bowling bowls in her hands.

"Take the shoes . . . and take me," he added softly. "Until death do us part."

Her head sprang up. "But—"

"No. There are no buts, Sunny. Not this time." He shoved a hand through his hair and huffed out an unsteady breath. "No buts and no Prince Charming either. Just a damn fool who loves you and wants to marry you and is doing a terrible job of conveying those points."

Blinking away her surprise, she let out a small, shaky laugh. "I don't know, I think you're doing a pretty good job so far."

"I can do much better," he said as he tenderly drew her into his arms. Right then and there, Sunny couldn't imagine anything better.

Feeling the small pressure of his jaw against her hair and the warmth of his arms, Sunny squeezed her eyes closed and relished the moment that she would remember for the rest of her life.

"I love you," Sam murmured into her hair. "I love you, and I almost let you walk out of my life because I was too afraid to admit it. I've been closed off, walking so long in the dark, I almost missed the light when it came back into my life. You're that light, Sunny. I can't let you out of my life again. Not now. Not ever."

Sam had said he loved her. Joy welled inside her as she tilted back her head to meet his eyes. "I love you too," she whispered. "And the children. So very much."

Sam wound her fingers through his and kissed her hand. "I know. And I won't ever doubt that again. Sunny, I may not be a prince, but if you agree to marry me, I'll make sure you're treated like the princess you deserve to be treated like."

"But, Sam, I can't move to New York. Not now. I'm going back to school in the fall to become a veterinarian. I've already received a scholarship. Are you sure this is what you still want?"

Sam smiled, his eyes crinkling with amusement. He slowly leaned forward, and his soft lips claimed hers in a long, deep kiss. She sighed against his mouth, totally content and convinced by his answer and the way their fairy-tale ending was playing out this second time around.

"Does that show you I'm sure?" he murmured against her lips. "My work can be done from anywhere. I don't need to be in New York. I need to be with *you*. Besides, I can't think of a better place to raise the children . . . together."

She chuckled and then lost herself in Sam's mouth again. After a long moment, Sam suddenly drew back, his eyebrows pulled together. "Hey, you know, you never did answer my proposal."